Dear Reader,

Anniversaries are usually happy occasions, whether celebrating births, marriages, or new beginnings. This month starts a happy celebration for Harlequin Romance— forty years of providing wonderful love stories that connect readers the world over. When you picked up this book, did you consider how many other people are reading it at the same time? Whether you live in England or Australia, Norway or Japan, Hungary or the United States, we share a common love of romance fiction. And we are able to indulge in this common love through Harlequin Romance.

Over twenty years ago I picked up my first Harlequin Romance book, to read while my baby napped. My children are grown, but I continue to be an avid reader of Romance novels—and have even managed to write a few. So join me in celebrating Harlequin's fortieth anniversary by curling up with another love story.

As you may suspect by now, Wyoming is a place near and dear to my heart. But Wyoming is not comprised entirely of cowboys. For *Angel Bride* I chose to show another facet of life in Wyoming with the story of a university professor and a hard-edged cop. For over two decades I've traveled the world through Harlequin Romance novels. I hope you enjoy traveling to this little bit of Wyoming!

Happy anniversary, Harlequin!

Barbara McMahon

P.O. Box 977
Pioneer, CA 95666-0977
U.S.A.

Angel Bride
Barbara McMahon

Harlequin Books

TORONTO • NEW YORK • LONDON
AMSTERDAM • PARIS • SYDNEY • HAMBURG
STOCKHOLM • ATHENS • TOKYO • MILAN
MADRID • WARSAW • BUDAPEST • AUCKLAND

A Special Thanks to:

Lieutenant Cliff Aims, for invaluable insight into the workings of the Laramie Police Department. To Jeff Mach, for explaining life at the University of Wyoming. To Tim Wilson, for all the information about cattle ranching in Wyoming. And to Cath Laing for all the wonderful work you did for Western Weddings. I miss you!

ISBN 0-373-03451-2

ANGEL BRIDE

First North American Publication 1997.

Copyright © 1996 by Barbara McMahon.

CHAPTER ONE

ANGELICA Carstairs looked up as he filled the doorway and her heart caught, her breath stopped. For an endless spiral down time, everything stood still.

He hadn't changed.

Yes, he had. He appeared harder, older, tougher. He'd always been big. Now, in the heavy winter coat, he seemed gigantic. He topped six feet by several inches. His broad shoulders still looked as if they could carry the weight of the world. Yet his size had never intimidated her. He'd always been heart-stoppingly gorgeous, with his sinfully dark hair and piercing black eyes. In that, at least, he hadn't changed. Neither had the stubborn jut of his jaw, or the intense manner he used to focus his full attention on someone to the exclusion of everything else.

He focused that attention on her. His eyes were cold, harsh, and peered right into her soul. Gone was the softness she'd glimpsed once or twice. Gone was the amusement that had often danced in the dark orbs. Now he regarded her as a stranger.

"Are you the one who called about the break-in?" he asked, his eyes flicking quickly to Martha Benson, her neighbor, back just as quickly to her, holding her gaze as if he'd never released it.

Angelica nodded, afraid to trust her voice. She hadn't expected Jake Morgan to respond to the police call. He was a detective, not a beat cop. Not anymore. Did he like his new job? Though she guessed it wasn't that new by now. He'd just gotten the promotion when—

"Here?" He glanced around the tidy living room, his eyes missing nothing. Coming back, they studied Angelica.

She shook her head and slowly rose. Tearing her gaze from his, she smiled politely to Martha.

"Thanks for letting me wait here. I'll let you know what they find out," she told her neighbor.

"Okay, Angelica, come back if you don't want to stay home alone tonight." Martha and Sam had let her use their phone to call the police. They had insisted she wait with them for the police. Angelica had found the front door to her house forced open. A quick glimpse had been enough for her to see her living room had been trashed. Fleeing to the safety of her neighbors without entering her own place, she had called the authorities from their phone.

Clearing her throat nervously, Angelica stepped closer to Jake, smiling politely at Martha as she passed to lead Jake to her place. Agonizingly aware of every inch of the man, she was extremely careful to refrain from even brushing lightly against him. It wasn't easy. She longed to feast her gaze on him, drink in the very sight of him. It had been over two years since she'd last seen him. Two long, endless, lonely years. But she schooled her eyes forward and focused on the doorway leading to the cold winter night.

She tilted her chin in a parody of confidence, hoping she could fake it enough to fool him. A woman had to cling to some pride when a man dumped her. Especially when she never knew why.

"I live two doors down," she said as they reached the cleared sidewalk. Snow had been piled high on the curb when the snowplows had done their jobs. The small mound bordering the walkway on the lawn side looked insignificant in comparison. Most of the row houses were dark. Part of a large complex on the outskirts of Laramie, all were fairly new. Angelica had been thrilled when she found she could afford one of the smaller units. It was a safe neighborhood; she would never have expected a break-in. And not in her house. She had nothing to tempt a burglar.

Their footsteps crunched on the icy sidewalk, their breaths hanging suspended before them in vapor clouds of pale white. Despite the freezing temperature, Angelica's blood heated from proximity to the man walking so closely beside her.

"When did you discover it?' Jake asked, falling into step beside her, careful to keep a certain distance between them. His steps were measured, deliberate. He moved smoothly, almost predatorially. He always had. She remembered feeling protected by it once. Now it seemed faintly threatening.

"I got home about seven tonight. I spent Christmas with Rafe and Charity. When I reached my front door, I could see it had been forced, the lock broken. The door was slightly ajar, not much. It didn't register at first. What it meant, I mean. I pushed the door and turned on the lights before I saw the mess. Then I went to Martha's to call the police."

"Smart. Never go into a house that's been burgled until you know it's safe."

He had told her that before, when he'd cared about her, worried about her living alone. He had told her many things to keep her safe. Only he hadn't been able to tell her anything to keep her heart safe from the devastation and pain he'd caused when he stopped calling.

"I remember," she said softly.

"Damn." His voice was so low she wasn't sure he really spoke.

"Are you back on a beat?" Angelica asked as she hesitated before the open door of her town house. She hated to go inside and see the damage that had been done. She'd been so proud of her home; now all was in chaos. Stalling wouldn't change anything but maybe it would help her cope a bit better. And she needed help if she had to deal with seeing Jake again, as well.

"No. I was on my way home when the call came in. I swung by just to check—on the off chance the guy might still be here. The regular patrol should be here in a minute or two." Jake pushed past her to examine the destruction in the living room.

He stood still and let his eyes roam around the room. She knew he recognized some of the furniture from the apartment she'd lived in when he'd known her. Other things were obviously new. He studied them for a long moment. Everything was tumbled in turmoil, but the rampant destruction so common with vandals was not evident.

"How long were you gone?" he asked, walking farther into the room, throwing a quick glance at her, then looking away. He didn't want to look at her. Didn't want to see how pretty she looked in her burgundy sweater, her long, slender legs encased in black wool pants. Didn't want to notice how her honey blond hair gleamed in the bright overhead light, longer now than when he'd known her. He especially didn't want to look into her sky blue eyes. He'd been lost once before in those eyes. Never again!

He didn't want to be within a mile of her, if the truth be known. He clenched his teeth. The sooner the beat cop showed, the better. This was strictly business. What had passed between them was best left in the past.

"I was gone six days," she said, her eyes wide as she stared blankly at the mess.

"So this could have happened at any time over the past week."

He moved on to the kitchen. It hadn't been touched. The short hall to the left led to a bedroom and bath. The bedroom had been tossed, as well. He paused in the doorway, trying to assess the damage without touching anything. The large bed was new. He quickly moved his gaze. The room was full of feminine clutter that seemed so foreign in his very male world.

"My guess is it wasn't vandals but someone looking for money," Jake said as he reentered the living room. Angelica hadn't moved. She stood near the door, her expression bleak as she surveyed the scattered books, the jagged screen of her computer and the overturned tables and chairs.

"Looks like vandals to me. They smashed my computer."

"After we dust for prints, you can check the place out to see if anything is missing—"

"Hey, Morgan, slumming? I didn't hear there was a need for the big boys here. Thought this was just a routine B and E." A tall man in uniform stood in the doorway, smiling.

Angelica turned suddenly at the new voice. Relaxing slightly, she watched as the beat cop entered and introduced himself as Pete Winston.

"Pete. Just stopped by. I was on my way home and heard the call. Thought maybe the perp might be nearby, but this could have happened as long as a week ago." Jake moved easily toward the door, his manner undergoing an immediate change.

Angelica watched avidly as he relaxed, the friendship with his co-worker evident. It was a sharp contrast to the cool remoteness with which he treated her.

"What happened?"

"Don't have much. Angelica Carstairs is the victim. Came home from a trip and found it like this." Jake shrugged, his gaze surveying the room once more, pausing only briefly on Angelica's face.

"I'll take over now, thanks. We'll see you at the New Year's Eve shindig, won't we? You bringing Diane?" Officer Winston drew a leather-covered notebook from his pocket.

Angelica's gaze swung sharply to Jake.

He nodded as he headed for the door. "Yeah. Save us a seat if you and Heather get there first. See you." Without another word or another glance at Angelica, he left.

Angelica watched him leave, her heart throbbing heavily in her chest. Her breathing was still erratic. She tried to blame it on the disruption to her life by the break-in. *Diane*. She closed her eyes briefly, wondering if the pain would always be with her. *He was seeing someone else*. Should she have been surprised? He was the most decidedly male individual she'd ever known. And she'd known plenty. Raised on a ranch not too far from Cheyenne, she'd been surrounded by macho cowboys and wranglers from birth. Her two older brothers were both strong, virile men. But Jake had them beat six ways to Sunday.

He'd probably been dating all along, ever since he'd last called her. But it hurt. Damn it, she had loved the man, adored him, thought he walked on water. She'd even started to believe he cared for her.

Then presto, one day he didn't call. And never had since. No explanation, no easing down. Nothing.

"Sorry you have to go over everything again, Miss Carstairs, but if you could fill me in on what happened, we'll see what we can do." The police officer held a pen poised.

The night seemed endless. The questions were easy, but she knew very little. Once the fingerprinting had been taken care of, she was permitted to set her things to rights. While doing so, she tried to determine what, if anything, was missing.

But her concentration did not focus on her task. It centered squarely on Jake Morgan. As she had endless times before, she wondered what had happened to end their relationship. She'd been crazy about the man and had thought, in his own way, he'd been crazy about her.

Granted, he had never been as demonstrative as she. In his line of work, trust and frivolity came rarely. He had seen things she'd never even dreamed about. But there had been a spark between them, a growing closeness that she had cherished. Where had it gone wrong?

"Nothing much is missing," Angelica said in wonder as she put the last pillow in place on her bed. The police officer dogged her footsteps through every inch of her place, asking her again and again to verify nothing had been taken.

"Nothing?" He sounded baffled.

"I can't find my backup diskettes, but nothing else is missing. Not that I can see. And the only things really damaged were my computer and the two books where the spines were broken." It could have been so much worse.

"Hello?" A voice called from the front door.

Angelica followed the policeman to the living room, peering around him. For a second, she thought Jake had returned. Instead, a locksmith stood in the open door.

"I got a call that you needed emergency repairs tonight," he said genially, his hand already running down the damaged door near the broken lock.

"Yes, I do, as you can see. Who called?" Angelica rubbed her forehead. She would have to get the lock fixed before she'd feel safe going to bed. Thank goodness the man was already here.

"Some cop called." The man shrugged, examining the splintered wood where the lock had given way. "I can fix this right up for you. Won't take more than half an hour." With that he set to work.

"That's it for me, then, Miss Carstairs," Officer Winston told her some time later. "I'll call you if I find out anything or have any more questions. If you discover anything else missing, let me know."

"Thank you." Angelica sank down on the sofa while she waited for the locksmith to repair her door. The policeman had checked all the other doors and windows for her; nothing else had been tampered with.

She felt violated. Her home, her sanctuary had been invaded. It would be a long time before she would feel comfortable here, knowing some stranger had been through her things.

When the door had been repaired and the locksmith had left, Angelica continued to ramble around her place. She hated to turn out the light—which was stupid. The house was secured, and whoever had trashed her place was long gone with no reason to return. All the damage had been done.

The phone rang, sounding unnaturally loud in the stillness of the night.

"Hello," she said, snatching it up. Anything to postpone going to bed.

"You all right?" The familiar voice seeped through her like fine whiskey, deep and dark and a bit rough. How many other nights had he called late, when he'd gotten off a shift and wanted to speak to her? She closed her eyes and let the bittersweet memories flow through her.

She swallowed, old longings rising fast and hot.

"Yes. Thank you for checking."

"The locksmith finish?"

"Are you the one who called him?" A warmth flooded through her at his thoughtfulness, even as tears pricked behind her lids.

"No big deal. You have a lot on your mind with this, I'm sure. It's not your normal welcome home."

"No. Thank you. I wouldn't have thought about it until I was ready to lock up. This way, the police officer was still here when he arrived so I had someone with me the whole time until the door was secure again."

"Anything missing?"

"No." She couldn't let it end there. In only seconds he'd hang up. And it would probably be at least another two years before she saw him again or talked to him. Or maybe there'd never be a next time.

"I didn't expect to see you tonight," she said, longing to keep the lines of communication open if only for a few moments longer. She wanted to lap up his deep voice, to relish the shimmers of excitement from hearing it. If nothing else, it chased away some of the fear.

"I didn't know you moved. Last I knew, you still lived over on Sheridan Avenue."

"I moved about eighteen months ago." Had he known, would he have ignored the call? Let the other cop be the first on the scene? She was afraid to ask him, afraid of his answer. "Are you still at the same place?"

"Yeah. Listen, I'm glad your door got fixed. Chances are the guy broke in the first night you were away and has been long gone since then. You'll be fine." He became more impersonal, more distant.

"Yes." He was reassuring them both she'd be safe, then he'd pull away like before. And she still didn't know why.

"Call 9-1-1 if you hear anything or get scared."

"Yes. I—" There was nothing else to say. "Goodbye, Jake. Thanks for calling."

Angelica woke the next morning after a restless night's sleep. It wasn't only the break-in that had kept her awake; it was seeing Jake again. She dressed warmly in dark wool slacks and a bright blue sweater, then brushed her long hair until it crackled with static electricity. Toast was all she wanted for breakfast. And coffee. She didn't feel much like eating.

As she sipped her second cup, she wandered back to her living room and stood almost where she had last night. She could picture Jake there, prowling around, looking for clues to assist in apprehending the person who had broken into her place. Curiously she wondered what he'd thought of her home? Had he connected it to her at all in any personal way? Or was it just another crime scene to him?

And who was Diane? How serious were they? Would he stop seeing Diane as suddenly as he had stopped seeing her, or was he more serious this time?

Shaking her head impatiently, Angelica finished her coffee and briskly began to make plans to contact her insurance company, replace her computer and clean her house from top to bottom to get rid of all the fingerprint powder. She'd put Jake Morgan behind her two years ago. Seeing him briefly last night wasn't going to miraculously change anything.

The house shone when Angelica finished and she was pleasantly tired. Surely tonight she'd sleep.

Tomorrow she'd have to begin her lesson plans. After destroying her computer hard drive, the vandals had then absconded with her backup floppies. As the newest assistant professor of mathematics at the University of Wyoming, she had prided herself on being prepared. She had mapped out her courses during the past summer and had thought herself on top of things. Now she was back to square one. Or square two anyway. Some of her preliminary notes were in her office at the university. Tomorrow she'd go pick them up. At least she had a starting point.

The knock on the door was unexpected. Nervous, she hesitated and used the peephole for the first time. Recognition was instant.

"Jake?" She opened the door, startled to see him again. After two years of silence, twice in two days?

"Hi, Angel. Can I come in?"

"Sure." She stepped back, her eyes fastened on him. There was no way she could stop the spontaneous curl of heat that seeing him ignited, but she could control her reactions around him. Pasting a polite smile on her face, she took a deep breath and held it, trying desperately to look as remote and detached as he did.

"Everything's back to normal, I see," he said, standing near the sofa. He dominated the room, his very presence seeming to fill it with excitement and masculine power.

Angelica nodded, afraid to step too close lest she be scorched by his heat.

"Anything missing?"

She shrugged. "They broke the computer and stole my diskettes. Other than that, nothing. And it's such a pain. I had all my lesson plans on the computer. I have to start over and classes begin again next week."

"Tough break. But it could have been worse. Does Pete suspect it was kids looking for exams or grades or something?"

She shook her head, wishing she could step away. His eyes were dark, searching, seeking. She hoped he didn't see more than she wanted him to see. "I don't keep exams here. I've already turned in the grades from last semester. I don't keep anything important from work here, just lesson plans."

He shrugged, his eyes never leaving hers. "Students don't necessarily know that."

"Maybe at the beginning of each school year I should announce that to all my classes," she said lightly, suddenly wishing she could bring a hint of amusement to those assessing eyes, a hint of softness to the hard glare that never deviated an inch.

Instead, he merely nodded. "Might be a good idea."

She shook her head and relaxed as much as her racing heart would allow. "Want come coffee?"

He hesitated a long moment, as if weighing the pros and cons before finally nodding slightly.

"I'll get it. You could take off your coat if you're staying awhile." She hurried to the kitchen, feeling as fluttery as a freshman dating a senior. What was the matter with her? He was an old friend. *Friend*? Well, more than that, but if she didn't want to set herself up for future heartache, she'd better remember he hadn't wanted it that way and had ended it.

So why was he here?

Jake shrugged out of his heavy coat and tossed it across the back of her sofa. Prowling around the room, he loosened his tie as a further concession to comfort. He'd had a twelve-hour day and was tired. But he wanted to make sure she was all right before he headed for home.

He paused by her desk and studied the wrecked computer. Whoever had damaged it had wanted to make sure it would never work again. The monitor had been bashed in. The processing unit had been smashed, circuit boards bent and broken, the hard drive mangled beyond recovery. Was there a reason, or was it just wanton vandalism?

Slowly he turned, his glance taking in the rest of the room. It was warm and welcoming. As Angel had been the entire time they dated, warm and welcoming yet just a bit wary around him. Moving on, he stopped by her bookshelves, smiling at all the mystery titles.

She'd always been a mystery buff. Once, a long time ago, he'd wondered if that was why she had liked dating a cop. He hadn't thought about that in a long time.

He spotted a group of photos. Her brother, Kyle, he recognized instantly, his expression tightening as his gaze moved to the next photo. The man looked a bit like Angelica in a rugged way. He must be her brother, Rafe. Was the petite woman with him his wife? The faded picture to one side had to be her parents, the couple who had died when she'd been a little girl.

"So why did you come, Jake?" Angelica asked as she stepped into the room and deposited the tray of coffee carefully on the table in front of the sofa.

"I wanted to make sure you were all right," he said, turning and crossing the room to sit on the chair near the table.

"You could have checked with Officer Winston. Isn't he the one in charge? He could have told you I'm fine." She handed him a cup, sweetened and black. She remembered how he liked it.

"There's fine and there's fine. I wanted to make sure," he repeated, watching her over the rim of the cup as he took a sip. It was hot, but not as hot as she made him feel. Coming here had been a mistake.

"Actually, I'm more angry than anything right now. I'm incensed that someone had the nerve to break into my home. Furious that they touched my things, destroyed my work. And irate that I don't have a clue as to who did it so I could hold them accountable," she said, flaring up.

"Better anger than depression or fear," he said. She was pretty when she was mad, her eyes like blue flames, her cheeks rosy and flushed.

"Fear? Oh, about staying here, you mean?"

He nodded.

"I guess." She sighed heavily, calming slightly. "There's nothing to do but go on." As she had when he stopped calling. She'd tried to call him a couple of times. But when she'd been given the runaround, she'd known not to call again. Gripping her hands tightly around her mug, she sipped her coffee. She ached to know what he had been doing these past two years, longed to know if he had missed her at all. But she refused to ask a single question lest she never be able to stop.

Jake stood abruptly. "Thanks for the coffee. I'm glad you're doing okay after all." He grabbed his coat when she stood.

"Thanks for stopping by." She tilted her chin again, as she had the night before. She would not break down and beg him to stay. He had made his decision two years ago. Why, she still didn't know, but it didn't matter. He was no longer hers. He never had been.

Despite her best attempts, however, when she opened the door, her hand brushed against him involuntarily. Her fingers skimmed his sleeve, feeling the rock-hard muscles bunch tightly. She closed her eyes briefly at the shock of sensation that flooded through her.

"Take care, Angel," he said huskily as he passed by and out into the cold night. No kiss, no hug, no words of future meetings. Simply *take care*. Yet it was more than she had received last time.

Drifting off to sleep later, Angelica was vaguely pleased to acknowledge she'd not revealed any indication to Jake of how much his leaving had devastated her. She ignored the loneliness in the big bed that she had once thought to share with a hot, passionate male. She was over him. Or she would be one day soon. Very soon! She had lesson plans to worry about now, not some tall, rugged cop.

Wyoming enjoyed a clear spell. The last storm had been prior to Christmas and the forecast continued clear and cold. The snow hadn't melted, but with the roads plowed, it was as good as it got during late December.

Angelica bought another computer first thing the next morning. She had another week before classes began and she needed to work flat out to make sure she was ready for the first day. Her job as assistant professor in the mathematics department had been hard won. She would make sure she performed so well that there would never be any question that the decision had been the best the university had made. She had her eye on an associate professorship before she reached thirty.

After purchasing the computer, Angelica headed for the university. Fall classes had ended before the Christmas break, but there were still students wandering the campus, some working on a thesis or long-term projects, taking advantage of the vacation days to catch up. Others were just hanging around for any action they could find.

Angelica smiled as she made her way to her office. Only a few years ago, she'd been an undergraduate. How she'd loved it. So much that Rafe had once accused her of wanting to become a professional student. But it wasn't so. She liked the synergy of the university. She'd made the switch from student to instructor then assistant professor with no trouble.

The office building echoed eerily when she entered. The usual crowd of professors, instructors and endless groups of students was missing because of the holidays. Even the administrative staff was gone until next week. Her footsteps rang in the oddly silent building.

She hurried up the stairs to the small cubicle she called her home away from home. It had a narrow window that gave a brief glimpse of the distant mountains. Scarcely large enough for her desk, bookshelves, large chalkboard and a couple of chairs, it still represented the first step up the ladder toward a full professorship. And she was lucky enough to have it all to herself.

Angelica opened the door and stopped dead.

CHAPTER TWO

"I'M TRYING to reach Detective Jake Morgan," Angelica said yet again. This was the third voice to come on the phone. How hard was it to get through if someone had an emergency? Or was he deliberately avoiding her? Was he worried she'd call him on the slightest pretext to try to insinuate herself back into his life—

"Yeah, this is Morgan." His distinctive Western drawl was more welcome than she anticipated.

"Jake, it's Angel. I'm sorry to bother you at work and all, even though it is police business. Well, it's really probably more for Officer Winston, but I don't think his beat extends over here and the campus police did say they'd handle it and contact the city police, so I—"

"*Angel!*"

"Yes?" She took a deep breath, holding on to her nerves with a will of iron.

"Take a deep breath and slowly tell me why you're calling. Slowly." The order came through loud and clear.

Angelica took another deep breath. "I did. I thought I did. Jake, my office was ransacked like my house."

"I'll be there in ten minutes," he said, severing the connection.

Slowly, Angelica placed the receiver carefully back on her phone. She tried a shaky smile for the elderly

22

security guard standing beside her desk. "He's coming over," she said.

"Campus police won't like it, miss. They said they'd handle it," the man said morosely.

"Yes, well, Detective Morgan is a friend, a personal friend." And she was beginning to feel she needed one. It was cold in her office. And the scattered files and folders, torn papers and ripped books added to the chill. She stood and headed for the door. "I'll wait outside for my friend," she said, not waiting for agreement, giving in to a need to escape.

She sat on the marble bench in front of the building, willing the rays of the brilliant winter sun to warm her. Cool, crisp air swirled slowly around, cold enough to keep the snow from melting, to keep the sun from offering any solace beyond an illusion of warmth. Still, she felt better sitting outside than in her office.

Soon she'd have to go back upstairs and clean it up. She hoped she could find her notes for the spring classes and that her grading sheets and student files weren't impossibly scrambled. But for the moment she just wanted to sit in the sun and forget the scenes of destruction that had met her eyes ever since her return from Christmas vacation.

Jake careered around the corner in front of the student union. He drew to a halt before the Ross Building, against the flow of traffic, his light flashing. Climbing from the car, he immediately headed for her, as out of place on the college campus as a fox in a henhouse. His tall frame moved easily through the scattered groups of undergraduates with a controlled motion that reminded Angelica of a lobo wolf on the prowl. King of the wolf pack, dominant, arrogant, confident and deadly, he made the strutting college boys look like pups. Yet he remained totally oblivious to it, his eyes already on her. All his attention focused on her.

Willing her heart rate to slow, Angelica sprang up from the bench and waited impatiently for him to reach her. She couldn't take her eyes away from his dark gleam. For one heartbeat she felt safe. Jake would find out what was going on and make things come right. She knew it.

Then the shivers of awareness began, raking through her as he drew nearer and nearer until she could reach out and touch him. But she didn't have to. He reached for her first, drawing her up firmly against his hard chest, holding her in his arms while she breathed out a shaky sigh of relief, resting her forehead against his shoulder.

"Oh, Jake. I know it isn't your case and I probably should have called Officer Winston, but I wanted you. I didn't know what else to do."

"You're shaking." His arms tightened even more until she could feel the steel in him along the length of her, feel the imprint of masculine strength surround her.

"It's the last time I take a trip, I can tell you," she said, trying for some humor. Truth to tell, she felt just the tiniest bit scared.

"Where's your office?" He released her, held her shoulders while he ducked his head to stare down into her blue eyes. "Do the campus police have any ideas when it happened?" he asked, ever the cop.

"They don't know. Some time since school let out. It's this way." She felt momentarily bereft when his hands dropped from her shoulders, but one arm came around her and she leaned against him, savoring his strength. Drawing on her own determination and courage, she led the way inside and to her office.

The elderly security man stood on duty, leaning against the brick hallway wall. Except for the door to Angelica's office, all the others on the floor were closed.

"This is Detective Morgan of the Laramie Police. He wants to see my office," Angelica said as they drew abreast of the open door.

"Now, mister, there's no need. The campus police have been and gone. They have the case in hand," the older man protested.

Jake smiled easily, offering his hand to the guard. "I'm not planning to run interference, just checking it out for Miss Carstairs. I won't touch a thing."

"I'm sure that won't matter. The place has been dusted, pictures taken. She can clean it up now if she wants. I'm just waiting around until she's ready to leave."

"Nice of you. I can take over if you have other things to do," Jake offered.

After a sharp look at Jake and a quick glance at Angelica, the older man nodded. "You'd probably do her a whole lot more good than me if there was a problem." He nodded and saluted Angelica with two fingers before heading down the hall.

Jake swung back to her, the smile gone, his expression pure business. "Let's see."

She stood aside as he prowled her office. Since the campus police had already dusted for fingerprints, he had no hesitation in picking things up and examining them.

"Anything missing?"

She shrugged. "Not at first glance. But it will take days to get this mess cleaned up and put back into order. Much longer than it took at home if they've scrambled the papers."

"Any other office hit?"

"No. The campus police checked when they were here."

He leaned back against her desk and stared around the small room for a long moment, then snapped his gaze toward her.

"All right, let's have it, Angel. What do you have that someone wants?"

"Nothing!"

"A break-in at home and one at your office in the same week. That stretches coincidence a bit too far. You must have something someone wants pretty badly."

"I don't." She glanced at the mess again before peering thoughtfully at her computer. Unlike the one at home, this one had not been damaged. "But someone might think I do, I guess," she said slowly.

"Like what?"

She hesitated. She knew she could trust Jake with her life, if necessary. But she wasn't sure how much she should tell anyone until she'd spoken with her boss.

"Actually, I need to talk to someone else."

"What the hell do you mean you need to talk to someone else? You called me the minute you ran into trouble. Now you want to talk to someone else? Who?"

"I can't say." She swallowed hard. Tension grew as he stared down at her; she could feel the sparks. She should have anticipated this and, as a precaution, should have called to get clearance. At the very least, she should have notified them what had happened. Only she'd never considered that anyone would think she had classified materials with her.

"Isn't it a little late to be thinking about the boyfriend?" Jake snarled.

"Boyfriend?" She blinked. Was that a joke? She hadn't had a date in over two years, and he thought she had a boyfriend? And why would he care if she did? He'd made it abundantly clear he no longer wanted to be considered in that role. And what about Diane?

He reached across and grabbed her arms, drawing her up close. His dark eyes were hard and narrowed as he leaned over until his nose almost touched hers. "I'm the one you called first, sweetheart. I'm the one who can help you, not some boyfriend you only just remember now."

She blinked, feeling the soft kiss of his breath fan across her cheeks. Her gaze took in the deep depths of his eyes accented with the faint lines that radiated from the corners, the high bones of his cheeks, the tight control he held on his mouth.

She licked her lips, wishing he'd kiss her once more as he had long ago. If she reached up a scant four inches, she could brush her lips against his, taste him again, absorb the searing heat he generated against her skin for another second of eternity.

"It's classified," she squeaked, drawing on all her reserves to keep from moving that short distance. Shimmering waves of desire swept through her. Blood heated through her veins and the roar in her ears almost deafened her. For years her brothers had tried to give her everything she wanted, but she'd never wanted anything as much as a single kiss from this one man.

Time hung suspended as the world narrowed to only Angel and Jake, blue eyes staring deep into black ones. Their hearts pounded in sync, their breaths mingling, uniting as one.

He moved first, straightening and setting her back. Waiting only long enough to make sure she hadn't lost her balance before releasing her, he stepped away, arching one eyebrow.

"Classified?"

She nodded. "About a year and a half ago, I was hired by the Strategic Air Command to do contract work in cryptography at Warren Air Force Base," she said, referring to the air base near Cheyenne.

"You crack codes?"

She smiled at that. "More along the lines of enciphering than deciphering. It, uh, goes hand in hand with math."

"And you think someone might be looking for these codes in your possession?"

"Which is really stupid. I wouldn't take anything from the site, much less leave it carelessly around my house or office."

"Maybe whoever is behind this doesn't necessarily know that."

"Then they can't be too smart. I think it's more likely to be your student theory. But I suppose I should check in and let my boss know what's happened."

"How often do you work there?"

"It's on an as-needed basis. I finished my last assignment just before Thanksgiving. They haven't called me for the next one yet." She moved around him and reached for the phone.

"How did you start working for them?" he asked, leaning back against the wall and crossing his arms as he stared across her office out the window.

"How? There was an invitation to the university, an ad sort of. I applied and they ran a background check and then hired me."

"When?" His gaze pierced her, his concentration formidable.

"Eighteen months ago." Suddenly she felt as if she were being interrogated. Why? She had done nothing wrong.

"Isn't that when you said you got your new place?"

"It was the extra money that enabled me to afford it." She frowned and dialed the number. Turning slightly for a feeling of privacy, Angelica went through the officer on duty and reached Colonel Shaefer. She quickly explained what had happened and offered Jake's theory of a disgruntled student as a possible explanation.

"Well?" Jake asked when she hung up.

"He said to keep him apprised. For the time being, he's willing to let it stay in civilian hands. Especially since he knows nothing's been taken from the base."

"What happened eighteen months ago that caused you to change your life, get a new home, take on additional work? Bad love affair?" Jake asked softly.

She glanced up, then shook her head in defense. There was no way she would give him the satisfaction of knowing how much he'd hurt her when he left. No way would she give him a clue.

"Just time to change things. I need to get some order out of this mess. I probably shouldn't have called you. I think the security guard was correct. The campus police—"

His fingers covered her lips, stopping the flow of words. Angelica shivered, stepping back to break contact.

"I'll see you home. The building is practically deserted and I'm not leaving you here alone. Get what you need and we'll go. You can come back when the staff returns."

"I remember how bossy you could be," she mumbled, kneeling down to stack papers together, piling them in such a way she could carry them home. She'd spend the evening sorting and trying to restore order. And there were still the lessons to plan.

"Bossy? This coming from the prima donna herself, who expected every man she knew to jump through hoops pleasing her?"

"That's not true." She flashed him a sassy grin. "If the man in question wanted to jump, who was I to stop him?"

Jake's smile hit her like a lightning bolt. Slow and sexy, it spun her senses until she was reeling. She reacted as if he'd touched her. She found herself smiling back at him as she felt the strong pull of physical attraction between them. He practically oozed masculine appeal. He was too potent to just spring on someone. She needed time and space to work up a resistance strong enough to withstand that blatant virility.

"Yeah, well, maybe your breathing makes men want to jump."

"Right." Dragging her gaze away, she stacked more papers. *That's why you left two years ago.*

"What are you planning to do with all those?" he asked, stooping down to her level.

"Take them home to sort. I can't start work next week with this mess. I need to get it all in some kind of order before school starts again."

"Wait until the staff gets back."

"No, I can get a lot done over the next few days."

"Tomorrow's New Year's Eve."

"So?" she said. Remembering Diane and the date she'd heard confirmed, Angelica wished he hadn't mentioned it.

"So what are you doing? A hot date?"

She shook her head, keeping her gaze firmly on the pages she was sorting. Her face grew stiff trying to hold a neutral expression. She should *not* have called him.

His fingers reached for her chin and tilted her head to face him. "No hot date?"

"No date, hot or otherwise," she said in a whisper. If he said one disparaging thing, she'd dump the stack of papers on him and storm out. It was no longer any of his business what she did with her nights.

His thumb gently caressed her lower lip, brushing back and forth slowly as his eyes tracked its journey. "Angel honey, he isn't worth it."

She could scarcely think. His touch drove her crazy—crazy with longings, yearnings that evolved from deep within and clamored to be assuaged. "Who?" she whispered, mesmerized by the soft touch of his thumb, the heat from his body, the scent filling her nostrils. She wanted nothing more than to spend the rest of her life with this man.

"The bastard who hurt you. Don't hide away from things because of him."

She blinked and sat back on her heels, pulling away from his hand. He watched her warily. He hadn't a clue that he was the man who had hurt her! She couldn't believe it. He sat there and advised her against himself. She almost wanted to laugh. If she hadn't wanted to cry so much she might have.

Scrambling to her feet, she picked up the papers she'd already gathered. "You don't need to worry about me, Jake. I'm managing just fine. I like my life the way it is," she lied. She dumped the stack on her desk, then frantically gathered up another pile.

"Angel—"

"Really, Jake. I'm fine. Go on and have fun to-morrow with Diane." She closed her eyes in anguish. She hadn't said that, had she? Someone please tell her she hadn't said that. Oh, God, couldn't the floor swallow her up?

"How do you know about Diane?" His voice was cool.

"I heard it somewhere. I'm ready. If you'll just give me a hand to my car, I can manage from there. I'm sure I'll be all right at home. I have the new lock and the bad guys won't be coming back. There's nothing there they would be interested in and—"

His finger stopped the words again.

"I'll see you home."

Angelica remained silent as they walked down the deserted halls, conscious of her footsteps echoing loudly while she could scarcely hear Jake's silent tread. She thanked him politely as he held her car door open, then she slammed it shut and started the engine right away. She wanted to get home, close her door and be alone.

He stayed right behind her during the short drive home. He was out of his car and over to hers before she could gather up all her papers. He accompanied her up the walkway, never touching, yet seeming to surround her completely. In other circumstances, she would have welcomed his attentiveness. Now she wanted him to leave.

"Thanks for seeing me home," she said, refusing to look at him lest her feelings showed in her eyes.

"Call me if anything else happens," he ordered.

She shrugged. "What else could?"

"Call me!"

She took a deep breath, nodded for the sake of expediency in getting rid of him, her eyes firmly on the knot of his tie.

But when he captured her face in the warm palms of his hands, she was lost. He raised her up for his kiss, his lips warm and firm, moving in a long-remembered caress that excited and soothed, that inflamed and enticed. Angelica responded instantly, like gasoline to a match. Heat flared and consumed her. She wanted more, wanted to step into his embrace, encircle his neck with her arms and press herself against him in a mating as old as time. She ached with wanting him to open her mouth with his and plunge into the welcome she'd so gladly offer. She yearned for him to touch her with hot hands that would learn her secrets and teach her new ones. She wished he wanted her as desperately as she wanted him.

But he pulled back after a brief kiss, his eyes flickering, his expression giving nothing away.

"Happy New Year, Angel," he said.

She watched as he walked away, her heart pounding, her cheeks flushed and hot. She wished she had nerve enough to call him back. Yet she knew he wouldn't come. He'd left two years ago after all. Nothing had changed, so why should he? Slowly she entered her house.

Angelica spent the next two days sorting papers. She found notes for classes, grading sheets for students, drafts for journal articles all mixed together in the piles she'd collected. Sorting everything kept her occupied, kept her from thinking about Jake.

New Year's Eve she went to bed just after ten. Trying desperately not to imagine Jake and his date at some party, trying to pretend she didn't mind being home alone another New Year's Eve, she climbed into bed with a mystery she'd been wanting to read. It couldn't hold her attention. Finally she dozed off, murder mixing with dancing and Jake pursuing the killer and then her.

The phone rang. Blinking, Angelica awakened and reached for it. She frowned. It was after midnight. She'd fallen asleep with the lights on.

"Hello?"

"Happy New Year, Angel." The deep, familiar voice warmed her to her toes.

"Happy New Year, Jake," she said softly, closing her eyes to better savor the happiness that bubbled up at his call. "Where are you?"

"I'm at the policemen's ball. Where are you?"

"In bed."

"Alone?" he asked sharply.

She giggled a little, then caught her bottom lip with her teeth to keep from crying. "Yes, not that it's any business of yours. And you're with Diane."

"I'd asked her a while ago. She's just a friend, Angel."

She started, suddenly wide-awake. Jake was not one to give explanations. Why explain this? She would much rather have had an explanation two years ago. How did he expect her to respond?

"Is it a nice party?"

"As these things go. They start off fine, then the guys get down to talking shop."

"Is Diane with the police department?"

"You don't want to know about Diane, Angel. Were you asleep?"

"I was reading."

"A mystery?"

"Of course, what else?"

In the background, Angelica could hear someone call Jake. The woman's voice sounded full of laughter.

"I've got to go."

"Happy New Year, Jake. Thanks for calling."

Angelica hung up in total confusion. Why had he called? If he hadn't happened to respond to her call about the break-in, she wouldn't have seen him again. He hadn't said anything about seeing her socially. But it seemed a very personal thing, calling to wish her a happy New Year so soon after midnight. Especially when he was on a date with another woman.

Two days later, the university resumed classes. Angelica went to work early, anxious to get her office cleaned up now that the rest of the staff was back to work. The building resounded with the calls of students, the click of high heels, the stomp of boots. The bustle was common and comforting. She plunged into the mess, determined to get it all under control as quickly as she could.

Angelica glanced at the clock from time to time. She wiped her hands on her wool slacks and stared at the phone. She planned to invite Jake to dinner, to thank him for coming to her rescue, so to speak. As soon as she gathered enough courage to call him. The idea had come to her when she woke New Year's Day. She had wanted to call right away, but decided she had better think the invitation through first. She didn't want to make it seem more than it was, merely a thank-you for his help at her office.

Right. If that was all she wanted, she could send him a card. How long had she been staring at the phone? She darted another look at the clock. He would be at work by now if he wasn't already out in the field somewhere. No time like the present to call.

In a minute.

Finally, chiding herself for her foolishness and cowardice, she dialed the number. Taking a deep breath, she pinned a bright smile on her face, hoping it would help her sound carefree and casual when she issued the invitation.

"Morgan," he growled.

"Jake, it's Angel."

There was a moment's silence on the other end. "Another break-in?" he asked.

"No. Everything's fine. Actually, I was calling to invite you to dinner Friday night." She said it in a rush. Damn, she had meant to be calm and casual. Too late now. She held her breath, awaiting his answer.

The silence ticked by slowly. Angelica could hear her heart beat, slow, nervous, heavy. The bright smile faded. He was going to refuse. She wiped a damp palm against her wool slacks.

"I don't think so, Angel, but thanks," he said at last.

"Okay. It was just a thought. I meant it as a thank-you for coming over when my office was broken into. No big deal." Her throat ached with disappointment.

"It's part of the service, ma'am." He was all cop.

"Right. Nice to know Laramie's finest are so prompt when called for help. Thanks again." She slipped the receiver back on the phone before she made even a bigger fool of herself. She looked up at the ceiling, blinking furiously. She would not cry over the rejection. Going into the call, she'd known he probably wouldn't want to see her again, unless she needed a policeman, of course.

Slowly she rubbed the ache in her chest. She was used to it now. She'd had it in one form or another for two years. But it still hurt fiercely. And after his attention the past few days, she might have been excused for thinking he might come for a simple thank-you dinner.

The phone rang. She jumped at the unexpected sound and looked at it resentfully. Gathering up her notebook and purse, she let it ring as she headed out to her first class. She'd be early, but the walk would calm her down and she could get started putting some of the problems on the blackboard before the students drifted in. She had work to do; she couldn't be fretting over a tall, dark man who had already left her once before.

* * *

Where was she? She had just called. Had she not been at work? Jake slammed down the receiver. It was just as well. He had no business seeing her for dinner. It would remind him too much of other dinners they had shared, of other evenings spent together. Yet he'd heard the disappointment in her voice. He wouldn't have deliberately hurt her for the world.

CHAPTER THREE

ANGELICA recognized his car as soon as she turned into her driveway. What was Jake doing here? She thought he'd made his feelings very clear on the phone earlier. Now what? Something about the investigation?

Reluctantly she pulled up and stopped. What she really wanted to do was turn around and drive until she ran out of gas, but that was hardly a mature way to handle this. Taking a deep breath, she wondered if maturity was overrated.

He had left his car while she dithered and was at the door of hers before she knew it. Opening it, she shivered slightly in the cold air. The late-afternoon sun was but a memory; dusk was falling fast and with it the temperature. It would be another cold night.

"Angel."

"Hi, Jake. What an unexpected surprise. Was there something more on the investigation you needed? I thought Officer Winston was the one handling things. I assumed you filled him in on the situation at my office last week."

"Angel, shut up. You talk a lot when you're nervous, did you know that?"

She glared at him. Of course she knew it. But she didn't like that he'd also recognized the fact. "Why would I be nervous?"

"You tell me."

"If I was the tiniest bit nervous, it could only be because of all the problems recently. I mean, how often does a person have her house broken into and then her office. I was lucky to have my car with me or it probably would have—"

He leaned over and kissed her.

Her lips clung to his, all protestations forgotten. The cold faded and a delicious warmth pervaded. Slowly, as if in a trance, Angelica dropped her books and briefcase and purse. She slipped her hands up around his neck, pulling him closer.

His arms encircled her and drew her snug against his long length. His mouth moved against hers until she opened to him, reveling in the taste so long denied. When his tongue skimmed her lower lip, she moaned softly in supplication. She wanted more. She was spinning out of control and didn't care a whit. Her tongue met his, danced with his.

When he eased back a bit, Angelica realized her coat was open, as was his. They had pushed them apart to press closer. She had no desire to move an inch unless it was to close the gap he'd created.

"Don't be nervous around me." Jake's voice was low and seductive. His breath brushed across her damp lips, warming them in the rapidly cooling night air.

"Jake, I'm not nervous. I was merely saying—"

Again he cut her off with a kiss, deepening this one until Angelica forgot where she was, forgot what she should be doing. The only reality was Jake in a spinning universe that spiraled in wondrous delight. She strained to get closer, to offer him the same heady delights he provided. Her mouth moved against his, her tongue mating in a rhythm as old as time. Her hands threaded themselves through his thick pelt of hair, relishing the texture, testing the length.

His heat scorched her, made her coat superfluous. Gone was the numbing cold of the Wyoming winter; gone was the hard concrete beneath her feet. She floated on a warm, tropical cloud of blissful sensation. Shimmering waves of electricity sparked along her nerve endings, bringing remembered pleasure so long forfeit.

"It was always hot between us," Jake mumbled, lifting his hands up to cup her face, dropping little kisses against her lips, across her cheeks, tilting her face to trail kisses along her jaw, down her throat.

"It was always wonderful," she replied, eyes closed to better savor every stroke of his touch. She could go on forever. Could he?

"I didn't come for this," he said, moving back to capture her lips for another hard kiss. Was he lying to himself? He straightened and reluctantly dropped his hands.

Angelica blinked, crashing back to reality in a rush. Embarrassed at her ready compliance, she bent to retrieve her books and purse. Searching for her keys, she turned to head for the door, conscious of Jake only inches away. She couldn't look at him. Did he mean to imply she'd thrown herself at him?

"Just why did you come?" she asked as she walked to the door, her head held high. She would not apologize. He'd kissed her after all. She'd only gone along for the ride—for the dizzy, spiraling, heart-stopping ride. She still felt his warmth. Once inside, she shrugged out of her coat and hung it in the closet.

Jake pushed in with her, closing the front door firmly behind him. He watched her steadily with his dark eyes as she turned to stare defiantly back at him.

"Well?"

"I came to update you on the progress made so far," he said easily.

For some reason, Angelica wondered if that were true, or only a trumped-up excuse. Fleetingly she smiled, then turned. Wishful thinking on her part, no doubt. Jake had never had to trump up anything.

"I thought Officer Winston was the one in charge of this investigation." She sat down on a chair in the living room, gesturing to another for Jake.

He took the offered chair. Angelica noticed he didn't remove his heavy coat. He was obviously not planning to stay long.

"Pete is in charge. But he filled me in and I told him I'd be seeing you and could let you know."

"Why?" she asked again.

"Why what?"

"Why bother? Officer Winston could have done the job. I think you've made it abundantly clear we have nothing to say to each other. So why were you the one to come by?"

He ran his fingers through his hair and leaned forward, wanting to shake her for being so elusive, for being so damned pretty and sitting there practically ordering him out of her house. He wanted to rail at her for shutting him out, for being all he could not have. She'd invited him for dinner only a few hours ago; now she was as cool as the snow in the yard, as distant as the Tetons.

"We talked to the duty officer at the base and obtained a list of people who had an idea of what projects you worked on. We cross-checked with the university. Got another list. We've been investigating the names on each list to see if anyone needed quick cash and consequently might be interested in minor espionage. We're trying to determine who knew you had access to classified files, and that you'd be away for a week at Christmas.''

"Good grief, you're questioning all my friends?'' she asked in disbelief. "Why don't you put an ad in the paper? Anyone who knows Angelica Carstairs come forward and be suspected of—''

"That's enough, Angel! It's routine police work and so far has resulted in nothing. But I wanted you to know we're doing all we can to make sure we catch the man.''

"A telephone call would have worked.'' She rather thought she was going to be sick. He had just come by to update her on the investigation. She didn't know why he'd kissed her, but she would bet her last dollar he hadn't expected her to respond so fervently. She'd all but plastered herself to him, prolonging the kiss endlessly. She wanted to melt into a puddle of embarrassment. But she held on. She wouldn't give way until he left.

"I wanted to see you,'' he admitted.

"That wasn't the impression I got this morning on the phone.'' She looked away, remembering how hurt she'd felt at his rejection.

"Yeah, well, the reason I didn't want to come to dinner is I didn't want a scene like we just had on your front walk. There's no future in it.'' That much he did know.

What's wrong with me that you can't love me? she screamed inside. Gritting her teeth hard, she clamped down on the words.

"Have you seen anyone suspicious around the place, or around your office?"

"Officer Winston asked me that. No, I haven't. And I'll be sure to let him know if I do."

"Him, not me?" Jake asked, his voice whipcord sharp.

"He's still in charge, isn't he?" Just leave, she willed him. Just leave me alone once and for all. This was torture to be so close, to have shared hot kisses, and still hear him say they had no future together. What did he want from her? Blood?

Jake rose, towering over her. "Yes, he's the one in charge." Slowly he leaned over, his finger rubbing gently against her swollen lips. "I didn't hurt you, did I?"

She shook her head. *Not the way you mean*.

With an exasperated sigh, he straightened and turned to the door. "I can see myself out."

Angelica remained perfectly still. Her eyes watched him walk away. Her ears heard the door open, close. Her body felt the endless silence and stillness of her empty house. She was alone—again.

But Jake's scent still surrounded her. The heat he engendered still warmed her body. The tiny pulses of electricity his very touch brought still hovered against her skin. Closing her eyes, she imagined he was still there with her. She sighed. It was going to be a long night.

And so it proved. It was after midnight and still she couldn't fall asleep. Groaning in frustration she rolled onto her side. The scene between them earlier that evening echoed over and over in her mind. She couldn't forget how wonderful it had been to be in Jake's arms again. The pleasure she'd received in his kisses, the touch of his hands against her face, his fingers threaded in her hair burned in her memory. She yearned for more. Much more.

Bother! At the rate she was going, she'd still be tossing and turning at dawn. She had to get some sleep! She had a math section at eight in the morning, and those students were sharp. She needed to be on her toes to challenge them.

Flinging off her covers, she quickly rose. Maybe some cocoa or a brandy or something would relax her enough to fall asleep. What she really needed was to get her mind off Jake. But that didn't look likely in the next few centuries.

She padded silently down the short hall and reached the door to the kitchen at the same instant the window glass broke. Startled at the sound, she snapped on the switch by the door, flooding in the scene with revealing fluorescent light.

She caught a glimpse of a hand and arm, quickly yanked out of the window and then gone. Shock held her immobile for a long moment, then she flew to the phone to call the police.

As calmly as she could, she explained the situation to the dispatcher. He promised immediate help. Even as she hung up, she could hear the distant wail of a siren. Apprehensively she stayed by the phone, watching the kitchen door to see if anyone came through. She heard nothing but the blood pounding through her veins. She thought she'd scared the intruder away, but she wasn't sure. She yanked on her coat and stood by the front door, tense and alert. If anyone came in through the kitchen, she'd flee out the front.

Seconds later, heavy pounding shook the door. Angelica whipped it open and almost flung herself into the policeman's arms.

In less than half an hour, things were back to normal. The officer had temporarily patched the window, scoured the grounds for an intruder, written down her statement and posted a patrol to survey the neighborhood until morning. The disturbance had awakened the Bensons, and when they heard what had happened, they insisted Angelica spend the rest of the night with them.

Gratefully she accepted. For one brief moment, she almost called Jake. But firmly refusing to give in to the temptation, she resisted. Gathering up her things, she locked the door behind her, wondering if she should consider moving. If these break-ins threatened to become a habit, she would have to. She couldn't continue to live like this.

Snuggled down in the guest room of the Bensons' a few minutes later, Angelica seriously wondered what anyone could want badly enough to break into her house twice. She had no state secrets, no final exams, no jewelry. It was most perplexing.

Immediately following that thought came the speculation about what Jake would do when he heard about this night's adventure. She really didn't need his help. The other police officers in the city were all competent individuals. And a lot less threatening to her own stable well-being. He'd mentioned again last night that they had no future together. She'd do nothing but set herself up for a load of heartache if she continued to see him, no matter how she longed to do so.

Starting tomorrow morning, she'd stand on her own two feet again. And if she needed some help, she'd call one of her brothers. They'd be there like a shot.

With that resolution firmly fixed in her mind, she drifted off to sleep.

Her home looked the same the next morning when she returned to dress for school. Officer Winston caught her just before she left for the campus. He reviewed the report the duty officers had prepared and asked a few more questions.

"I'm not sure how safe it is for you to remain here by yourself. Do you have another place you can stay until we can find the intruder? Someone like a close friend or relative?" he queried as he prepared to leave.

"Do you really think I'm in some sort of danger?" Angelica asked.

"The perpetrator had to know you were home last night. That makes the entire situation more dangerous. It seems as if our guy is getting more desperate."

She nodded, still baffled by what anyone could want from her. "I have some friends I could stay with for a couple of nights. I can't move in with someone indefinitely."

"We'll see if we can get any leads from last night's attempt. Until then, Miss Carstairs, I'd suggest you find another place to stay for the next few nights."

The interview with Officer Winston made her late. And Thursdays were her heavy days. She dashed from the parking lot to her first class, feeling as if she was out of step with the rest of the world. The feeling lasted through the morning. Without the calm preparation time she usually enjoyed, it seemed as though she was constantly scrambling to catch up. And always at the back of her mind was the constant worry about the break-ins.

Grabbing a quick lunch, she wondered which of her friends she should ask for a favor. Sandy would be the best bet, not having any family to disrupt. Kyle lived too far away, plus her brother still acted as if she were a baby. She liked being independent. She didn't want to be under his overprotective thumb again. Yet Angelica wondered if leaving her place unattended would offer an open invitation to the intruder to try again. What could he want?

Angelica's last class of the day was advanced calculus for mathematic majors. She was well into the lecture, turning from writing a complex formula on the blackboard, when her eye caught the opening of the back door. Jake Morgan walked into the lecture hall and went to stand against the back wall. Angelica swallowed hard, losing her train of thought for a moment.

What was he doing here? She caught sight of the puzzled faces of the students, several of whom had turned to see what was causing her momentary distraction. Taking a deep breath, Angelica picked up the threads of her lecture and plunged in again. Feeling more vibrantly alive than just seconds before, she was aware of Jake's steady regard while she wrapped up the class for the day.

What was he doing here, and dressed as he was? He leaned negligently against the wall, wearing all black, from the dark boots and black cords to the thick black sweater that hugged his torso. He tossed a shearling jacket over the back of a seat, crossed his strong arms over his muscular chest and stared down at her.

Angelica could scarcely concentrate. He was far too distracting. She wanted to discuss some theorems, but couldn't remember which ones. She wanted to excite her students with the knowledge of the practical uses of calculus, but could only feel the excitement that being near Jake brought.

Finally, unable to concentrate, she dismissed the class ten minutes early. From the eager voices of the students, she had made their day.

Slowly the lecture hall emptied until only Jake and Angelica remained. She busied herself stacking the assignments that had been turned in and erasing the blackboard. Aware that Jake remained leaning against that back wall, studying her, she did her best to ignore him.

When the last student vanished, Jake pushed away and walked down the side of the room, his step measured and soft. Angelica turned to watch him approach, her heart beating double time.

God, he was dangerous. His dark eyes almost shot flames as they narrowed in on hers and held them captive. A muscle in his cheek jumped as he clenched his teeth. His broad shoulders were displayed to advantage in the dark sweater. The black cords encased long, muscular legs.

Her gaze dropped to his lips. Involuntarily she licked her own, wanting to feel his against hers one more time. God, how many one-more-times were there in life? Never enough, she was sure.

He stopped close to her, so close she could feel his body heat brush against her own, could see the thick lashes that framed his dark eyes, could smell the tangy masculine scent that was his alone. The scent that she would recognize anywhere, anytime. Something melted deep within her and she took a step closer.

She was like a moth attracted to flame. She knew she would get burned, but she couldn't help herself. She had to touch that heat.

"You're in big trouble, little lady," he growled.

Exhilaration spread to every cell in her body as his rough voice caressed her senses. Challenged, she flashed a haughty look and poked his chest with her forefinger.

"I'm not a little lady. I'm five foot nine."

He captured the finger and drew it to his mouth. Nipping it gently, he soothed the tip with his tongue. Angelica's legs grew wobbly. Slowly she inched closer to brace herself against his greater strength.

"From six-five you're not so big." He planted a hot, damp kiss in the palm of her hand, his fingers lacing with hers as he let their hands drop. Bringing them up behind her, he urged her the last few inches until her breasts pressed against his chest, her belly snuggled against his, her thighs felt the steel of his.

"But definitely a lady." Leaning over, he brushed his lips light against hers.

"Jake, you can't just come into my classroom like this and disrupt everything."

"Excuse me, Teacher, but I merely walked in and stood in the rear. I never said a word." His free hand wandered up to encircle her neck, his fingers gentle against her nape. His other arched her more firmly against him, holding her a willing captive.

"I . . ." It was true. He had done nothing but show up. All the disruption had been caused by her own reaction to seeing him. She was having trouble thinking. Pressed up against him so intimately, she was having trouble even breathing, let alone coming up with the fortitude to push him away.

His hand tilted her jaw, exposing her throat. With a soft groan, he lowered his mouth to that silky skin, kissing her, licking her, blowing gently on the damp skin.

Angelica shivered and shifted even closer, her free hand surrounding his waist, slipping beneath his sweater to press against his hot skin. Her breasts tingled with desire; heat pooled deep within her. Her legs remained wobbly, unable to support her weight.

"Why didn't you call me last night?" he asked, his eyes flashing down at her.

She blinked, tried to back away, but was caught fast by his arm.

"I told you to call me if anything happened. My God, how do you think I felt hearing from Pete this morning that there'd been another break-in?"

"There's no need for you to get involved." Disappointment raged through her. Had he only come because of last night's attempted break-in, out of some overextended sense of duty? "Besides, there wasn't anything you could have done that the policeman on duty last night didn't do. I spent the rest of the night with the Bensons."

"I sure as hell could have done something. Exactly what I'm going to do now," he said, releasing her and turning to the lecture desk. "This all your stuff?"

The sudden change was unexpected. Angelica nodded.

"Where do you want it?" He gathered up the stack of papers and folders.

"In my office, but I can manage them." She reached for them, but he was already heading toward the back of the hall. Snagging his jacket en route, he waited for her by the door. "Jake, I can manage," she repeated.

"Sure, you've done a great job so far. Let's go. We've got a long ride ahead of us."

"What are you talking about?" She almost had to skip to keep up with his longer stride. Throwing on her coat, she dodged a group of students and followed him from the lecture hall to her office.

He dumped her papers on her desk and turned to take her arm. "Let's go."

She dug in her heels and pulled Jake to a stop. "Wait a darn minute. Just what do you think you're doing? And where do you think we're going?"

"I'm taking you out of Laramie for a couple of days. It's too dangerous for you to stay around while some crook keeps breaking into your house."

"I'm not going with you. I was going to stay with Sandy for a couple of days—"

"Yeah, Pete told me he had you arrange to stay somewhere else. Call and cancel."

"I haven't arranged it yet, but I—"

"Good, then there's no problem. Need anything from here?"

"Hold it! I'm not going anywhere with you." Her mind boggled at the notion. Spend several days alone with Jake, no one else around? No matter how much the idea appealed, it would be emotional suicide. But she couldn't resist just hearing what he had to say. Nothing more.

"Where?" she asked.

That slow, seductive smile he gave so sparingly tilted the corners of his lips. Her heart caught fire. She'd walk through fire for those smiles.

"I have a place up in the mountains a couple of hours from here. We'll stay the weekend there. That'll give Pete and his men a chance to follow up on some leads without your being around."

"What leads?"

"We were lucky. You have a new mama in your complex. She'd just put baby to sleep when she heard the breaking glass. She looked out the window and caught a glimpse of the intruder. She was even able to give us a partial description of his car. We'll get him, Angel. We just need time."

"Then I'll be fine at home."

"No, you're coming with me."

He tugged gently and she went with him. Her thoughts churning, Angelica tried to decide the best course of action. The *prudent* course of action, not what her heart clamored for.

"We can't leave for the weekend. It's only Thursday," she protested, trying frantically to come up with convincing reasons his plan would never work. She dared not tell Jake how she felt. She had to be calm and rational about it all and come up with a sound reason to stay as far from him as possible.

"That was your last class, wasn't it?"

"Yes. But what about your work?"

"I'm taking a few days' vacation. I haven't had one in years so they owe me."

She was intrigued. "Why not?"

"Why not what?" He glanced down at her as they reached his car. "Will your car be all right here over the weekend?"

She looked around. "If I were leaving it here for the weekend, it would be, but—"

"Get into the car." He hustled her into his four-wheel-drive Jeep, leaned over to fasten the seat belt. For a long moment, he gazed down into her eyes.

"I'm not sure this is such a good idea," she whispered, weakening.

"I'll keep you safe," he promised.

"Will you?" He hadn't before. She'd been so hurt. And he didn't even have a clue. It was probably a good thing he didn't know how he affected her, but could she stand to have her heart broken a second time?

Forty-five minutes later, they were heading toward the mountains. Two suitcases in the back seat contained their clothes. Angelica had her briefcase containing two journals she wanted to read, but Jake had refused to let her take any other work.

They were well beyond the city limits before Angelica allowed the enormity of the situation to hit her fully. She was going away for the weekend with the man she loved. Yet he was only protecting her from an unknown intruder. When the man was caught, Jake would say goodbye and she'd once again be on her own.

But she had three days at least, maybe more. She could store up a lifetime of memories in three days. Smiling suddenly, she knew she could never have resisted. She had other options. Rafe would come stay with her. Kyle would have had her at the ranch. It wasn't that long a drive into Laramie that she couldn't have done it every day for a while. Or she could have stayed with Sandy.

The real reason she agreed to Jake's demands to go with him was that she wanted to. It was that simple. This time she knew there was no future for them. She wouldn't be caught unaware as she had been two years ago when he stopped calling. Now she knew she'd have to save up memories and be prepared to say goodbye when they returned to Laramie.

CHAPTER FOUR

THEY drove into the blinding afternoon sun. The sparkling snow reflected the rays until Angelica wondered how Jake could see to drive. She donned dark glasses and looked out the side window. The fields along the road were pristine and empty beneath their snowy covering. In the distance, she saw a small herd of cattle, but they had not trampled the snow near the road. For a moment, she was transported back to her childhood. She and her brothers had loved the snow, made snow angels, built forts, had rousing snowball fights. As the youngest, she had never won, but neither had she ever stopped trying. She tried to remember the last snowball fight. It had to be just before her parents had been killed. It seemed as if Rafe had changed overnight after that. Of course, he would have had to. He had been responsible for her and Kyle. Funny, she'd never thought about it before. How hard it must have been for him. He'd only been a kid himself.

"Worried about something?" Jake asked with a quick glance in her direction.

She turned, jolted back to the present. "No, just remembering when I was a kid, and the fun my brothers and I had in the snow. Doesn't seeing all this make you want to play?"

He shrugged. "I like some things in the snow. Skiing, snowmobiling. What do you mean by play?"

"Play in the snow itself. I loved making snow angels when I was little. My mom would come out and judge whose were the best. I always won." Angelica smiled in reminiscence. "Maybe because it was the only thing I could win. My brothers never gave an inch. And since they are both older, I didn't have a chance."

"They watch out for you," he said neutrally.

"Well, Rafe sure did. He kept me and Kyle with him after my folks died. But Kyle, too, started bossing me around after Mom and Dad were gone. Guess they took their responsibilities very seriously."

"Rafe is your older brother, right?"

"Yes, and he actually had custody of us until we came of age. But Kyle was bossier."

Jake darted her a quick glance and remained silent. He would say nothing. He knew how bossy her brother was, and how strongly Kyle felt about protecting his sister. Jake almost gave in to the temptation to tell her, as well, but the urge passed. It was old news. And Kyle hadn't said anything untrue. Jake wasn't the man for Angelica. Kyle had made that clear, but it would not have influenced Jake a bit if he hadn't agreed with the man. He had known Angelica had a crush on him. He had relished feeling special to such a warm and loving woman. But his way of life wasn't suitable for such a gentle woman, nor his background. She deserved much more. And Kyle had known it.

". . . sisters?" she said.

"What?" He'd missed the first part of her question while brooding on what had happened two years ago.

"I asked if you had any brothers or sisters? You never mentioned any when...before. But that doesn't mean you don't have any."

"I don't." His reply was clipped. He didn't want to talk about families.

Angelica studied Jake as he drove. He seemed lost in thought. When they'd been dating, he had sometimes been preoccupied, usually with a case he was working on. At that time, she had felt comfortable enough to ask what he was thinking. But not now. She wondered what he'd been doing the past two years, wondered about the crimes he'd investigated, wondered what he planned to accomplish by taking her out of Laramie for a long weekend. Was it only to keep her safe while the rest of the force searched for the burglar? Or was there more to it?

"I missed you these past years," she said bravely. "Did you miss me?"

He nodded once, briefly.

Her throat ached as she held back the words demanding to know why he'd stopped calling her, why he hadn't responded to her calls. But she couldn't voice the questions.

"Where exactly are we going?" she asked instead.

"My place."

"I didn't know you had a place in the mountains. Where?"

"Just above Centennial. I've had the land for a long time. A couple of summers ago, I built a small cabin. Some of the guys from work helped. Now I let them use it when I'm not coming up."

"Oh, Jake, how wonderful. I can't wait to see it."

"It's not much, just a couple of rooms. But the view is nice."

Twenty minutes later, he pulled to a halt before a small log cabin. The wide front porch was well sheltered from the snow, which drifted considerably deeper in the yard than it had in town. Angelica's eyes darted everywhere as she took in the building, then the fantastic view.

"Jake, this is beautiful." Her voice was hushed as she gazed in delight at the scene. "You must come up here every chance you get."

"No, I don't get up that much." Building it had been a way to keep the memories at bay. But once he had completed the work, staying at the cabin proved lonely. It reminded him too much of things that he couldn't have.

Angelica hopped out of the car, glad she'd worn warm boots when she sank to her knees in the snow. Reaching for her briefcase, she turned and trudged to the porch. Jake followed, carrying both their bags.

Nestled in the lee of the mountains to the west, the cabin was already in shadow. Dusk would follow shortly. Opening the door, Jake stood aside as Angelica stepped inside. She drank in the sight of his home, curious to see how he'd decorated it. It was Spartan, the furniture sturdy and practical. To the left of the doorway, she saw a long sofa before a stone fireplace with a couple of easy chairs flanking it. To the right, a large, scarred pine dining table sat surrounded by wooden chairs. Beyond was the open kitchen. A closed door split the back wall.

There were no curtains, no rugs, nothing to soften the stark lines. Angelica itched to bring a little color to the room, to warm it up with curtains covering the windows, comfortable pillows piled on the sofa, and a thick rug on the floor before the fireplace. But it wasn't her place to do so.

Neither, apparently, was it any other woman's place. For that she was curiously grateful.

"It's wonderful," she said, smiling up at him.

He looked around the room as if seeing it for the first time and shook his head. In comparison to the warmth and color of her place, it was barren, almost bleak. "Still not finished. But I'm not much on curtains and such. Maybe you have some suggestions." He closed the door and deposited their cases beside it. "I'll get a fire going. That's the primary method of heat. Don't take off your jacket just yet."

As Jake moved to the fireplace, Angelica dropped her briefcase on the sofa and went to gaze at the view through the front window. The cabin sat on the slope of a hill, with a small valley beneath it. The sunlight still shone on the opposite hill, the snow reflecting the late-afternoon colors of gold and pink. The worries about the break-ins seemed surreal in such a serene setting. Angelica sighed with pleasure and turned to watch Jake build their fire.

"You could almost commute from here," she observed, perching on the arm of the sofa.

"No, I prefer to live in town. If I'm needed, I want to be right there. This is fine for weekends and vacations."

"Yet you said you don't come very often. Why not? I'd think you would come up all the time and bring loads of friends with you."

"It's not big enough for load of friends."

"Then a special friend," she said as if probing a sore tooth.

He looked up and met her gaze. Slowly he stood, his eyes never leaving hers. "I've never brought another woman, if that is what you're hinting at," he said pointedly.

Pink washed up through her cheeks as he answered her not-so-subtle question. She should have been embarrassed, but her relief that he did not habitually bring up other women was too strong. She was the first! She wished she had had a hand in building it. Dare she take him up on his request to help decorate it?

She cleared her throat. "Why not?" she whispered.

He smiled and stepped closer. "There is only one bedroom." Reaching out his hand, he rubbed the back of his fingers over a heated cheek.

Her eyes widened at that. Did that mean...?

"Fortunately, the sofa opens out to a bed." Teasing lights danced in his eyes as he studied the myriad expressions crossing her face.

She wished she were as forward and brazen as she sometimes was in her dreams. She would love to be bold enough to step into his arms and say not to bother with the sofa bed, there would be plenty of room in his bed for both of them. But while wanton fantasies were fine for dream time, they did not have a place in real life.

He dropped his hand and shrugged out of his jacket. The fire had started, and already Angelica could feel some of its warmth.

"There are things in the freezer and cupboards. Let's see if we can find enough for dinner or if I have to go back to Centennial for some food."

Angelica trailed after Jake, shivering a little in the cold cabin, the temperature almost matching that of outside. How long before it warmed up enough to be comfortable? With the fire, the stove and the oven, it should be toasty warm quickly. She knew a shortcut. If he'd just kiss her once...

Even thinking about a kiss warmed her ten degrees. She unbuttoned her jacket and let it hang open.

Her eyes tracked Jake as he rummaged around in the cupboards and pulled out some cans and boxes. Then he moved to the freezer and searched through the frozen packages. Curling her fingers, she shoved her hands into her pockets to keep from acting on the urge to thread her fingers through his thick, dark hair. She spun around and gazed out the window over the sink, lest every private longing be revealed to Jake when he looked at her.

"That's it. Frozen steaks, boxed potatoes, canned corn." He looked up, a trace of uncertainty in his eyes.

Angelica met his gaze, touched. Was he worried about what she thought about dinner? She smiled.

"I can panfry the steaks, make gravy and biscuits to go with it," she offered, turning to take off her jacket.

He was right there, easing the thick coat from her shoulders, tossing it across a chair, raising her chin with the edge of his hand.

"I remember your gravy and biscuits. They were always great."

"I'm glad you liked them. Men are so easy to please. Cook them a hearty meal, plenty of everything, and presto, instant satisfaction." She smiled saucily up at him. Feeling alive for the first time in two years, it was glorious.

"I remember your saying that once before, when we had that barbecue." He hesitated a moment, then murmured, "I remember everything you said." His eyes searched hers, roaming over her face as if memorizing her features.

Angelica was struck dumb. *He remembered everything she'd said?* Then why—

"And I remember how mouth-watering good your cooking was. So I'm accepting that offer before you change your mind." Jake brushed her lips lightly with his and turned away. "There's another fireplace in the bedroom. I'll build a fire there so the room will be warm when you go to sleep tonight."

"I'll take the sofa," she said, watching him with some bewilderment. He'd kissed her, then turned away as if he'd just brushed off a pesky fly. What was the matter with her? Hadn't she at least mastered kissing?

"You're my guest. You get the bed." He strode from the room before she could muster any arguments.

Angelica turned to the counter and began to prepare the meal. She didn't really mind sleeping in his bed. It would probably be the only time she would get the chance. And who knew what her fervent imagination would come up with?

She was in the midst of cooking when Jake returned. She put him to work cutting out the biscuits and placing them on the baking sheet. While she kept a careful eye on the gravy, he whipped the potatoes. They worked well together, almost as if they'd worked in harmony for years.

Moving around each other as they performed their tasks, Angelica felt as if she were participating in an intricate dance. She and Jake passed, reached around each other and sidestepped out of the way, each time drawing closer and closer. Once she stopped dead and he bumped into her, carrying a bottle of wine and two glasses. If her hands hadn't been full of plates and forks, she would have reached up to touch his cheek. He stood so close his breath caressed her cheeks.

"You must be warm enough. There's color in your cheeks and your eyes are bright blue," he murmured, refusing to move. She had stepped in his way deliberately. If she didn't want to be there, she could step around him.

"It's the cooking." *And your proximity!* She leaned ever so slightly forward. Deliberately she ran her tongue over her lip and dared him to ignore her.

"Now if we do this very carefully, neither one of us will drop anything," he said, encircling her with his arms, holding the wine bottle so it didn't spill. The empty wineglasses clinked gently as his arms drew her in and his face lowered to hers.

His lips were warm and firm, moving across hers in a lover's caress. Angelica sighed as she held herself stiffly, afraid to drop plates yet unwilling to step away from heaven. She relaxed and savored his touch. Opening her mouth for his gentle assault, she was assailed by tremors that consumed her. She had lived in a desert of emotions for so long. The glorious feelings that shimmered through her were thirst-quenching. She had never known such love before and knew she would never again experience this with another. Jake was the only man for her. She wasn't sure what had gone wrong between them, but it had nothing to do with this. Nothing could compare. In this they were as compatible as two people could ever be.

Slowly he raised his head, ending the kiss. Angelica was pleased to note his breathing was as erratic as hers. At least she wasn't the only one feeling something. But could she get him to admit as much? Get him to explain why he'd dropped her? Get him to consider some kind of relationship with her now?

"Is the meat burning?" he asked.

"Oh!" She whirled and slammed the plates on the counter, then snatched up the pan and pulled it from the burner. Great! Just when she needed to make a good impression, she burned the food. Gingerly lifting the edge of the steak with a fork, she noted it was only slightly scorched. Salvageable, at least. Was her relationship with Jake equally salvageable?

In short order, they set the table and served dinner. Jake ate as if he hadn't eaten in a month, steadily, without talking.

"Were you that hungry?" she asked at one point. He could put away as much food as either of her brothers.

"I was hungry, but more for your cooking than anything else. I get tired of eating out, or eating my own attempts."

She toyed with her wineglass, the deep red burgundy reflecting the flickering firelight. "So what have you been doing these past couple of years?" she finally dared to ask. Heart pounding, she hoped he wouldn't refuse to answer. She longed to know everything he'd done, everyone he'd met, every place he'd visited. She only wished she had been able to do it with him.

"Working mostly. Built this place."

"But no vacations."

He shrugged. "I took time to build this." And glad he had been to have this project. "Though I know it doesn't look finished. Any ideas about curtains and things?" he asked.

She glanced around the large, open room. "I could make some suggestions. Don't you have someone else you would rather have a hand in this?'' What of Diane? she wanted to scream. Just who is that woman and what is she to you?

"Your house is a good example of what I'd like. It's—friendly, I guess.''

She smiled, warmed that he liked her home. She'd spent a lot of time fixing it up to suit her. She hadn't had much else to do.

"A weekend doesn't offer enough time to do a lot, but I'll think about it and try to come up with some ideas.''

"Do more than that, Angel. Decide what it needs. Next week we can go shopping in Laramie, then bring everything out next weekend.''

"If you want me to, I will.'' Her heartbeat sped up. He planned to spend time with her during the next week and bring her back next weekend. That didn't sound merely like guard duty, keeping her from harm while the police found the perpetrator.

"Okay.'' She could scarcely contain her delight. She'd be with him for the next few days! As recently as her drive back from Rafe and Charity's, she had never expected to see Jake again. She'd been reminded this past Christmas of all she was missing when in the presence of her older brother and his petite wife. Now that they had the baby, Angelica was even more envious.

Jake and Angelica did the dishes companionably; she washed while he dried and put away. It didn't take long for the two of them to finish. When he handed her the dish towel to dry her hands, she grabbed each end and tossed the towel over his head, pulling him toward her. His arms went easily around her as if they had been embracing for years.

"What do you want?" he asked huskily, pushing her back against the counter, holding her securely in his arms.

She opened her mouth to tell him exactly what she wanted, what she had wanted for two years, but nothing came out. Heat stole up into her face, and butterflies danced in her stomach. She swallowed hard and squeaked out, "Coffee?"

"In front of the fire?" he asked, his voice low and sexy, his eyes dark and intense as he gazed down into her flushed face.

She nodded, her hands gripping the towel, resting against his solid chest. Held in his arms, she felt more feminine than ever before. He towered over her, an uncommon event in her life. Except for her brothers and one of the ranch hands on the family spread, Angelica usually met most men eye to eye.

"Do you still like sugar in it?" she asked, slowly releasing one end of the towel and pulling it from around his neck.

He nodded, releasing her. Taking one hand, he separated her fingers and held one up. "Just dip this in the cup and it'll sweeten it enough." Then he kissed the tip, drew it into his mouth and wet it with his tongue.

Angelica leaned against the counter, thankful for its support. Her legs felt like jelly, her heart thudded and the heat that washed through her made the fire superfluous. Tears stung her eyes. He'd said that so many times before. She'd forgotten. How could she have forgotten? It had been such a special joke between them.

"Hey, what's wrong?" he asked, one thumb rubbing just beneath her lashes, capturing a tear.

"Nothing, I just was remembering." She tried a wobbly smile. "You used to say that a lot."

"You were always the sweetest thing I ever knew," he said so softly she almost didn't hear him.

When Jake planted a damp kiss in the center of her palm, she instinctively closed her fingers over the spot, sheltering it. Turning on shaky legs, she reached for the coffee. His mouth grazed against her hair. He gently pushed it aside and she felt his lips brush her neck.

"You're making it somewhat difficult to concentrate," she said, her voice trembly. "Do you want coffee or not?"

For an endless moment, he didn't answer. She longed to turn and see his expression, but too afraid of what her own might reveal, she refrained.

"Yes, I want coffee." So saying, he straightened and walked into the living room.

Angelica chanced a glance toward him as she poured the ground coffee into the filter. He added wood to the fire until it blazed. She felt the heat clear across the house. Her eyes moved to the bedroom. Was the fire in there as warm?

"I need to change the sheets," Jake said, standing and heading for the bedroom.

With a glance at the coffeemaker, Angelica headed for the bedroom, as well. It would be several minutes before the coffee finished brewing.

"I'll help."

The bedroom was almost as large as the living room. The windows reflected back their images of the night. It definitely required curtains. Angelica didn't like feeling so exposed after all that had happened recently. The sooner he got curtains, at least for this room, the better, as far as she was concerned. Funny, before the incidents with the break-ins she hadn't minded an open window. Would she feel more comfortable once they'd caught the man?

Together they made the large bed. The headboard held reading lamps, and Angelica wished they were going to bed together. It would be fun to slip beneath the thick pile of covers, read for a while, then turn—

"The bathroom is through there. I should have told you earlier," Jake said, interrupting her thoughts and nodding toward the open door. "The hot water heater is propane. As you know from doing the dishes, we have plenty of hot water. You can take a bath or shower, if you wish."

"I'll wait until morning, if that's okay with you." Patting the pillow one last time, she skirted the bed and headed for the kitchen. Safety in distance right now, she thought, hoping she could resist the urge to draw him down on the bed with her and hold on tight until morning.

The delicious aroma of fresh coffee filled the living room. Angelica poured their cups, added cream to hers and sugar to Jake's. Carrying the cups carefully to the sofa, she placed them within easy reach and sat down. It was cozy before the fire. Drowsily she gazed into the dancing flames. She always liked staring into fires, watching the different images the flames suggested.

Jake came in and dumped a pile of bedding on one of the chairs. Sitting down beside her, he reached for his cup.

"This is nice. I don't have a fireplace in my house. That's one thing I really regret about it," she murmured, sipping from her cup.

"Cutting enough wood to last the winter can be a pain, but I think it's worth it every time I come," he said.

They sat quietly for a while, sipping coffee, watching the fire. When Angelica finished hers, she placed the empty cup down on the floor. When she sat back up, Jake reached for her hand, threading his fingers through hers, resting their linked hands on his thigh. He continued to sip his coffee silently.

Angelica leaned back on the sofa, her only anchor to reality her touch with Jake. Idly she daydreamed. She was full, warm, happy. For the first time in a long long time, she felt totally content.

"Tell me about your house." Jake broke the silence. "When did you buy it?"

"I bought it about eighteen months ago. I had gotten the part-time job at the air base and had enough money. I can use the tax break, too."

"I used to see you riding your bike sometimes," he said lazily.

Turning her head on the back of the cushion, she looked at him. "When?" She hadn't seen him in two years. Yet he'd seen her?

"In the spring. One time during the summer."

"I was probably going to work. That's one advantage of the town house, its location. I can ride my bike to the university in nice weather. Even walk if I want to. I didn't see you."

"Unmarked cars. I would have thought you'd be married by now."

Startled, she shook her head. Why would he have thought such a thing? Had her feelings for him been so nebulous to him that he thought she'd gone on to another man as soon as he was out of the picture?

Had she seemed too anxious for marriage? Was that the reason he'd pulled back?

Angelica tried to remember if she'd ever done anything to give him the feeling she was desperate for marriage. Two years ago, she'd only been twenty-four. Granted, she had talked a lot about Rafe's marriage to Charity, but surely Jake hadn't thought she was trying to pin him down to popping the question.

Although if he'd asked her, she'd have accepted in a New York minute.

"I have no plans to marry," she said.

He put his cup on the floor, released her hand and gently clasped her wrist. With his other hand, he began to trace her fingers with his. Idly playing with her hand as he leaned back on the cushions, he turned his head toward her.

"That's not the way I heard it." Even now he could feel the familiar anger rise. Kyle had been blunt and frank. Yet Jake had known even then that Kyle was right.

"I might marry one day. But I have no plans now." She pulled her hand free and scooted a bit to the left, putting distance between herself and the disturbing man who sat so close to her. She didn't want to talk about marriage when the only one she would ever consider marrying didn't want her.

"But you had plans two years ago," he persisted.

Now she would die of embarrassment. How had he known of her foolish daydreams? Had she given herself away? For weeks she had dreamed of making a life with Jake. Had he known all along?

Rising, she scooped up the two cups and headed for the kitchen. "A lot of things have changed since then. I don't think my future plans concern you. Don't worry that I'll hang around once you find whoever is breaking into my place. I've managed fine on my own and will do so again." She stormed into the kitchen, placing the cups in the sink with exaggerated care, afraid she might turn and smash them against the wall, so great was her embarrassment and frustration.

She should have called Sandy and insisted on staying with her. She knew she was playing with fire in coming with Jake, but she hadn't been able to resist. She had not expected him to bring up her foolish daydreams about marriage. She had thought she would be spared that, at least. She thought she had been the only one to know.

"Angel..." He followed her into the kitchen.

Glancing over her shoulder, she stepped to one side, giving him as wide a berth as she could.

"My name is Angelica. Only my family and close friends call me Angel," she lashed out, hurt and humiliated.

"Friends is what I thought we were. Until..."

Until you wanted more. If he had shouted the words, she could not have heard them more plainly.

"I'm tired. I'm going to bed. I'll be finished in the bathroom in a few minutes if you want to use it then."

Keeping the table between them, Angelica crossed to the bedroom door and closed it behind her. She went into the bathroom, gritting her teeth to keep from crying. How could anything so wonderful be so painful?

Jake slumped against the counter, his eyes still on the closed bedroom door. What had happened? Obviously she was still hurting from the man who had deserted her. He smiled mirthlessly. Hadn't her brother Kyle been able to salvage the relationship once

Jake had stepped out of the picture? That must have been frustrating for Kyle. Jake ran his hand through his hair. Kyle had nothing on him in the frustration department!

CHAPTER FIVE

BY THE time Angelica was ready to face Jake the next morning, she had herself firmly in hand. She had not slept well, but that was becoming a habit since she'd started seeing Jake again. Trying to live down her behavior of the previous day would prove a challenge. She decided as soon as she awoke that she would not let herself forget for a single moment that she was here only because the Laramie police thought it safer than staying home.

There would be no more tossing a towel around Jake's neck and pulling his face down for a kiss. No more suggestive remarks leading to comments about her fingers being sweet as sugar. If he wanted coffee, he could get it himself. She would remember the real reason for her presence in his house and behave accordingly.

Angelica believed all the admonitions she'd given herself until she walked into the kitchen and saw Jake. Instantly, every thought flew from her head.

He wore only jeans.

She swallowed hard. It wasn't fair. She had had the best intentions in the world when she left the bedroom, but that was before she saw all that expanse of bare skin. His shoulders had always been broad. Now they gleamed, muscular and enticing, in the early sunlight that shone through the uncovered windows. The light dusting of dark hair on his chest looked silky. She longed to brush through it to ascertain exactly how soft it really was. The sleek muscles in his back bunched and flexed beneath his taut skin as he scooped coffee into the filter, stretched to fill the carafe with water.

She swallowed hard, her eyes tracing over every mouth-watering inch, her fingertips tingling, heat rising.

"Aren't you cold?" she asked abruptly. He needed to put on a shirt before she lost what tenuous control she held. When he turned, she knew she was done for. He was gorgeous in the only way a perfect man can be. His hair was tousled, sexy as hell. His cheeks and chin bristled with day-old beard. When had she developed this longing to rub against that stubborn jaw, to feel the scratchiness that covered the hard cheekbones? Such a compelling urge proved almost impossible to resist. She actually took a step closer before she caught herself.

"I'm not cold. I thought the fire had warmed the place up," he returned. "Are you cold?"

She was hotter than billy blue blazes, but it had nothing to do with the fire in the fireplace. The blame could be squarely laid at his feet. She glanced down. Even his feet were bare. Closing her eyes, Angelica took a deep breath. Opening them again, she forced her gaze to meet his. Ignoring the tempting expanse of male flesh only a few feet away was nothing short of miraculous. She was proud of herself.

"I'm not hot, but I am wearing more clothes than you." Blast! She had not meant for her voice to crack.

He looked at her oddly. "I was waiting my turn in the bathroom. I'll take a quick shower. There's not much for breakfast. Oatmeal, maybe?"

"That's fine."

"Are you all right?"

"Yes, why?" She couldn't breathe. How long could a person live without breathing?

"You look as if you're in a trance or something."

"I'm just looking you in the eye."

He frowned.

Sighing in defeat, Angelica let her gaze roam over the decidedly masculine body that stood before her. Slowly she licked her lips and stepped closer. "You know, Jake, you probably should go get that shower now," she said, reaching out to touch his biceps. His skin was warm, smooth, taut. Lightly she skimmed her fingertip down his arm, feeling its silky texture change to the light roughness where darker hair covered his forearm.

"Yeah." But he didn't move. Then he did. Only to step closer, draw her up against that wide, enticing chest and lower his mouth to hers.

Angelica moved eagerly into his embrace. His scratchy beard abraded her softer cheeks, but she didn't care. She opened herself for his kiss, welcoming him, reaching for him. His tongue slipped into the soft moistness of her mouth and increased her heart rate a hundredfold.

Angelica encircled his shoulders, her fingers, palms, arms, rubbing against the bare flesh that tantalized her so. Relishing in the sensations, she wanted the embrace never to end. Slowly her fingers learned him, seeking to discover every nuance of his skin before sanity returned and they pulled apart.

His mouth made love to hers as never before. He demanded and offered, took and returned. His hands cupped her head, holding her where he wanted her as he sipped from her lips, plunged again and again into the sweetness that waited for him.

When he lifted his head, Angelica wanted to rush outside and plunge into the nearest snowbank to cool the blazing heat that threatened to consume her. Her lips were warm—the air cooled them. Her body was hot—nothing cooled it. Locking her gaze with his, she refused to release him. Her arms had a mind of their own.

"I've got to take a shower," he said, his hands brushing through her soft hair. His eyes were distracted as he watched the silken locks drift over and over between his fingers as he continued to comb through.

"I'll make breakfast."

He smiled down at her, his eyes dark and shadowy. Nodding slowly, he lowered his head again. This time the kisses were feathery light. Just a touch of his lips against hers. Not nearly enough to assuage the burning need that threatened to overwhelm her. Angelica stood on tiptoes to increase contact. He smiled against her, his lips moving over hers, yet denying her the full satisfaction she sought.

Remembering too late her own admonitions of only a few minutes ago, she pulled away. Clearing her throat, she tried for a reasonable tone. Shimmering waves of excitement tingled through her. Reasonable was not at all how she felt.

"Go." She stepped around him and stared at the coffee, trying to drag her raging emotions under some semblance of control. She would never make it through the weekend if she didn't maintain some decorum. Though who wanted decorum when they could have Jake served up practically naked first thing in the morning?

It was like playing house, she decided a little later as the sound of the shower ended. They had never even spent the night together before this weekend. Now they were living together. Not in the full sense of the word, but close enough to know how it would be. And as far as she was concerned, it would be great. They got along fine. They had some interests in common, and some different. But in the past, and during the last two days, they had spent endless hours together without any cross words. And she had never been bored around him. Could he say the same?

A thought struck her. Did she bore him? That could explain—

"Is this a new thing with you, going off into a trance?" Jake asked, walking into the room.

She spun around. Disappointment swept through her. He'd dressed. He wore faded jeans and another dark sweater. He had on black socks, no shoes yet.

"No, I was just thinking. Jake, do I bore you?"

"What?" He looked startled. Shaking his head, he chuckled. "Honey, the last thing you would ever do is bore me. I can't keep up with you. Where did that notion come from?"

"I was thinking that you don't bore me and I wondered if I bored you. Do you like brown sugar on your oatmeal, or cinnamon?"

"Sugar, of course. You have never come close to boring me, Angel."

She dished up breakfast and watched him from beneath veiled lashes as he ate. She liked playing house.

"I thought we could take out the snowmobiles after we ate," Jake said as he poured himself a mug of coffee.

"That would be fun."

"You've ridden snowmobiles before?"

"Sure. We have some at the ranch. Sometimes Kyle and Rafe use them instead of horses to reach some of the outlying ranges to check cattle. I've ridden them many times when I went along to help."

"Good. We'll go down to Centennial if you like and get some food for the weekend."

"Okay." Spending the morning in the cold air and snow would be the best thing for her. Get her mind off Jake. Then when they got back, she would read her journals, maybe make soup or something time-consuming for dinner. She had three days to get through before they'd head for home. She had to find things to keep her busy or go crazy.

Snowmobiling provided a perfect solution. Cold and windy, the crisp morning proved a total antidote to the heat that had suffused her. Glad for the change from the cabin, she snuggled down in her parka, knowing she'd warm up as they traveled.

Following her host, Angelica was able to indulge her craving for Jake. She watched him to her heart's content. As he led the way, it took only a couple of minutes before she knew she was in the presence of an expert. On her mettle to prove her own ability, she followed right behind him. If he could do it, so could she.

It was exhilarating! The swirl of snow that shot from beneath the traces spun like sugar in the bright sun. Rainbows and dazzling sparklers reflected back the variety of crystalline snowflakes. The sky was so blue it almost hurt. The air was so clean and clear it seemed almost as if she were breathing pure oxygen. She laughed aloud in sheer happiness.

They reached the general store in Centennial and left the snowmobiles neatly parked beside the larger cars. She giggled at the picture their two conveyances made.

Jake snatched off her cap and watched as she shook her head free in the frosty air. "Your hair is just as blond in winter as in summer," he said, handing her the cap.

"That's because it's still sun-bleached. I don't wear a hat when I ski so the sun can still get to it." Pleased he commented on it, she wanted him to notice every single thing about her. Something would click. She couldn't be the only one to feel so strongly in this relationship.

When Jake scanned the area before heading for the store, Angelica shivered. Instantly she was reminded why they were there. He looked like a cop now. All business. He had her with him to guard her, make sure she stayed unharmed. It was easier to forget when it was just the two of them, but being in Centennial brought it all to the fore.

"Jake, I'm not being stalked. Someone broke into my house and office," she said, stepping closer. No matter what, she felt safer near him.

"Old habits die hard, honey. Come on, what shall we get for dinner tonight?"

They took the scenic route home, passing a couple of places that afforded a magnificent view of the plains with the skyline of Laramie in the distance. One spot offered a spectacular panorama of the Snowy Range Mountains in all their winter beauty.

The groceries had not yet been put away when the phone in the cabin rang. Jake reached for it. He glanced at Angelica, turned slightly and kept his comments brief. Angelica paused a moment, then continued storing the food they'd just bought, shifting the supplies around in the cupboards. She listened with half an ear, but was unable to make heads or tails of the conversation from his cryptic comments.

When he hung up the phone, his face was grim. The call reminded him why Angelica was there. It wasn't a romantic weekend getaway. He was keeping her safe from danger.

"What now?" A tremor of fear raced through her.

"Someone broke into your car. The campus police called this morning."

"I shouldn't have left it at the college." Her legs felt shaky. Weakly she drew out a dining room chair and plopped down on the hard seat.

Jake whipped out the chair next to hers, turned it around and straddled it, stacking his hands on the high back. He rested his chin on them and studied her.

"Maybe we've been going at this wrong, Angel. We need to find out who is doing this and why. I thought you must have something someone wants. But what would you have in your car? Now I wonder if it's just someone getting back at you. Have you made someone angry lately?"

She shook her head.

"How about not so recently, like a year or two ago, but for some reason they are only getting back at you now?" Was it possible *she* had ended that other relationship? Was that the reason for the break-ins—retaliation by a rejected lover?

She shook her head.

"Angel, there has to be something!"

"Well, I don't know what it is! I'm not working on a project for the air force right now. I don't leave my notes at home or at my office about that work—ever. The new semester has just started, so I don't have any tests or exams around that a student might be trying to see."

"The fall semester ended when?"

"We had finals right before Christmas."

"Could it be a student looking for grades?"

She shrugged. "At this point I don't know who it could be. But I turned in my grades before I left for Rafe and Charity's place at Christmas."

"But would students know that? Could it be that simple?"

"Simple or not, I want it stopped. What happened to my car?"

"Passenger window busted. He took care to sweep away all the glass, too. If someone hadn't walked right by it and noticed the window was open, it might not have been discovered so quickly. No one leaves their windows open in this kind of weather."

"So he's been to my house twice, my office once and now my car. Should I leave a sign around that I don't have whatever it is he's looking for?"

"Tell me about the men in your life." He didn't want to hear what she had to say, but if it provided a clue, he needed to know.

The change was abrupt. Taken aback, she stared at Jake. Gone was the laughing rider on the snowmobile. Gone was the sensuous lover of that morning. Instead, she viewed a hard-eyed cop, intent on discovering any and all facts he could to solve a crime.

She wondered if she were still a person to him, or had she become just another case?

"There are no men in my life," she said evenly.

"Come on, Angel, not so. You're too pretty to be alone. Who have you been dating recently? Who do you go out with for coffee at work? What student has a crush on you?"

The last thing she planned to do was let this man know how his leaving had impacted her life. She simply would not open herself up to that. Tilting her chin, she glared at him. "First, I don't have any students who have crushes on me. Not that I know about. Wouldn't I be able to tell?"

He shook his head slowly. "I don't know. They might love you from afar."

"Right. Next, I have a friendly relationship with others in the mathematics department. But no one there is pining away over me. It may have escaped your attention, but I am no femme fatale."

"Honey, you are as pretty as the sunrise, as I'm sure you've been told many times. What you might view as only friendship, another might wish to change."

As she had with Jake. He had considered them friends when she had wanted so much more.

"Damn it, Angel, I'm trying to help you here and you're as closedmouthed as a clam. Tell me what I need to know!"

She stood up and slammed her fists on her hips. "I've told you everything I know. No one has a crush on me. I have no secrets at home. There is no man out there wreaking havoc in my life to get back at me for some imagined wrong. How many ways do I have to tell you that? I think it must be some deranged maniac targeting me for who-knows-what reason. But I don't know what it is, so stop asking me!''

She turned and stomped into the bedroom, slamming the door behind her. Her emotions were raw. She was a quivering mass of contradictions and need. She had begun to patch together her life after Jake had walked away so abruptly. Being around him now was no picnic. She wanted him as much as she had before, if not more. And the vibes she got from him were so confusing. One minute she began to think he cared; the next she thought she represented nothing more to him than a challenging case for the great police detective to crack.

Flinging herself down on the bed, she frowned at the ceiling. Not six hours ago, she'd told herself she would keep her distance from him. She would not be persuaded to fall into the trap of believing there could be anything between them. She needed to remember that. Jake had made his feelings in the matter perfectly clear. Why then did she have such a hard time accepting them?

The bedroom door swung open. Angelica glanced over to the doorway. Jake leaned against the jamb, his arms crossed over his chest. ''Don't sulk, Angel. It's unbecoming in a university professor.''

''Go away. I'm not sulking.'' She rolled over and looked out of the window. Just beyond the edge of the mountain, she could see the first traces of clouds. Was the weather changing?

''Give me some slack here, Angel. I'm not the bad guy.''

She rolled back and sat up at that. ''Neither am I, Jake, yet you hammer on me as if I were. I don't have the slightest idea who would be doing this. Don't you think I've thought about it until I'm numb? If I had any suggestions, I'd tell you. I want it to stop. Nothing like this has happened to me before and I don't like it.''

''I don't like it, either, and I'm only trying to figure out who's doing it.''

''It's not my fault.''

''I know that.''

''You don't act like it sometimes,'' she muttered.

''Just put it down to my being a sore loser, okay? I'll try to modify my tactics.''

''Take your interrogation *tactics* elsewhere. I'm not the suspect.'' She frowned. What did he mean by sore loser? Just because he hadn't found the burglar yet didn't mean he had lost.

He nodded, his eyes narrowed. ''Yes, ma'am. Come on, we'll drive into Laramie and take your car in for repair. It looks as if it might snow again.''

Slowly she rose and self-consciously smoothed the bed. Walking toward the door, she wondered if he was going to move out of her way, or would she have to brush by. At the last second, he stepped back, turned and led the way into the front of the cabin.

''My insurance is going to go through the roof,'' she complained as they climbed into the four-wheel-drive vehicle and began their journey back to Laramie. ''If they don't cancel me altogether.''

''When we catch the guy, we'll have him reimburse the insurance company. Relax, this kind of thing happens and insurance companies know it.''

''It doesn't happen to me. I've thought and thought until I'm blue in the face and can't imagine who would keep doing it or why.''

Jake reached over and took her hand, lacing his fingers with hers. "We'll find him and stop him."

Mildly comforted, she settled back for the ride. It did no good to worry. She had faith in the police force. Once they found the man, the break-ins would cease. And so would her reason to be with Jake.

She tightened her fingers, holding on for all she was worth. Their time together was so fleeting. She almost wished they would never find the man, that he would break in with great regularity, just so she could stay with Jake.

It was late by the time they had seen to Angelica's car. The clouds that had been peeping over the mountains obliterated the sun. The wind blew hard from the west, stirring up the snow, chilling the air. Angelica shivered as she climbed back into Jake's car.

"It's getting late. Want to eat here in town and then head back?" Jake asked when he joined her.

"Sure. Or we can go back to my place and fix spaghetti or something."

He hesitated. "We're having your house watched. I'd just as soon you not show up this weekend. If the offer is good at my apartment, we could eat there."

"Do you have more food at your apartment than you did at the cabin?" she asked suspiciously.

"No. But we're only a couple of minutes from the grocery store. We'll stop there first."

More playing house, she thought, walking beside Jake as he pushed the cart in the supermarket. She chose the ingredients she needed for a spaghetti dinner, remembering some of his tastes, learning a few new ones. Jake picked out a nice wine, and before long they were through the checkout and on the way to his apartment.

While Angelica knew where Jake lived, she had never visited. The apartment complex was one that was popular with students, close to the university and other amenities.

He led the way into the brick building, then down the ground floor hall to his door.

"Are you the only nonstudent here?" she asked as he slipped his key into the lock.

"No, Mrs. Fenster lives in 201. She's a widow who's lived here for years." Opening the door, he stood aside so Angelica could enter.

"Good grief, it's as cold in here as outside." Shivering, Angelica looked around.

The room was almost as sterile as the cabin. The only signs that someone lived there were the stacks of books tilted on one table and a couple of old TV guides that lay on the floor beside a recliner. The rest of the decor could be considered early bachelor. A place to hang his hat, that's all this apartment was. Where was his home? Where did he keep his pictures and memorabilia from the past? His bedroom, maybe?

"Yeah, it's cold. Just a sec, and I'll turn on the heat. I shut it off thinking we'd be gone for several days." He led the way into the minuscule kitchen and dropped the bag on the counter.

"Why is it so cold?"

"I leave the bathroom window open. I hate a stuffy place and this place is so old it seems stuffy if I don't have some fresh air."

"Even in winter?"

"With the heat on, it's warm enough."

"Your bill must be huge. You're heating up all of Laramie."

"It's worth it for fresh air. Come on, cooking dinner will warm you up."

"Oh, I see, this kitchen is much smaller than the one at the cabin, so only one person at a time can work in it." She paused at the door.

"Since you suggested dinner and are the better cook, I figured you could be the one person." He took her jacket, brushing his fingers against her neck as he removed it.

"It's your place. I really shouldn't intrude," she protested flirtatiously.

He frowned with mock ferocity. "You don't want to eat my spaghetti. You'd be awake all night from heartburn."

Instead of being awake all night from heartache, she almost retorted. Turning away from those knowing eyes, she began to unpack the grocery bag.

By the time dinner was ready, the apartment was warm. Jake had put on some soft music and drawn the drapes. They were cocooned in a world of their own.

They did not, however, linger over dinner. Jake mentioned that the weather report had predicted snow.

"And with the wind blowing the way it is, I don't want to be driving in a blizzard."

"We could stay in Laramie if it gets bad," Angelica suggested.

"No, I wanted to spend the weekend at the cabin. We'll make it back tonight. I just don't want to be late leaving here."

She didn't have to go back with him. She could still call Sandy, or Kyle for that matter. Considering all her options, Angelica sipped the wine. Its warmth crept into every cell of her body. Raising her gaze to

Jake, she knew she would return to his cabin with him. She was only pretending to herself that she would consider anything else.

The snowstorm hit before they reached Centennial. And, as Jake had feared, it was of blizzard proportions. The wind swirled the snow until visibility became almost nonexistent. The road was slick, treacherous. Even with the car in four-wheel drive, they skidded more than once.

"Can you find the cabin?" Angelica asked at one point. She felt as if they had been driving blind for an hour or more.

"Sure. We'll be there in another ten minutes or so," Jake answered easily.

"And then snowbound for how long?" she muttered.

"If it gets too deep for the car, we can always take the snowmobiles."

Just the thought of riding a snowmobile all the way to Laramie was daunting. She hoped the storm would be of short duration. A weekend at Jake's cabin was all she was prepared for. She had to be back at work on Monday.

True to his word, they pulled up before the log cabin a few minutes later. Rushing from the car to the door, Jake held on to her hand. Since she could hardly see him standing beside her, she was glad for the support. She might have lost her way getting from the car to the cabin.

Once inside, with the raging storm shut firmly behind them, Angelica relaxed. She had been as tense in the car as if she'd been the one driving. But they were safe at home now.

Home. She looked around at the familiar room. She hadn't felt such a sense of homecoming in a long, long time.

"We made it," she said softly.

"Home safe." He leaned over and kissed her.

CHAPTER SIX

ANGELICA closed the journal and gazed into the fire. She'd been reading all morning. Snow continued to fall steadily, though the wind had died during the night. The hushed air increased her sense of isolation. Idly she wondered where Jake had gone. He'd been fussing around the place when she began to read after breakfast, then mumbled something about checking on the snowmobile and left. How long ago had that been?

Caught up at last with her journals, she debated moving. She was warm and comfortable on the big sofa. The fire was dying, however, its feeble flames flickering as if they were gasping for air. She needed to replenish it to keep it going, but for the moment, she wanted to be lazy and not move.

There was so much that needed to be done. She had lesson plans to prepare. That had been the worst part about the break-ins, having her plans destroyed. She prided herself on being organized and ahead of the game. She also had a paper she wanted to submit to one of the mathematic journals, but needed to get her lesson plans finished before doing anything else. Yet all she wanted to do was find Jake and spend time with him.

Rubbing the ache in her breast, she remembered her determination to remain aloof, to refuse to give in to the emotions that flared whenever she came near the man.

Tough. She wanted Jake.

Rising, she tossed a couple of small logs on the fire, waiting until they caught before she replaced the screen and turned to the front window. Maybe she would offer some suggestions on how he could fix up this place after all. It was a beautiful structure and the furniture was good, if a bit austere. He only needed a few accessories to turn it into a warm and welcoming home.

And if she succeeded, he'd think of her every time he used his cabin. Smiling in satisfaction, she went in search of a notepad.

Angelica had a long list of things she wanted by the time she stopped to prepare lunch. She heated some soup, as well as the last of the French bread they'd bought in Laramie. When everything was ready, she went to find Jake.

He was in the shed, tinkering with one of the snowmobiles. A portable heater gave some warmth, enough that he'd taken off his jacket and rolled up his sleeves. His hands were black with grease.

"What are you doing?" Angelica asked as she slid open the door just enough to enter, then closed it quickly behind her to keep out the snow and chill.

"This was running rough yesterday. Thought I'd take a look at it. You finished your reading?" He didn't look at her but continued adjusting a valve.

"Yes, both journals. And I made a list of things for you to buy. It's fun, actually, spending other people's money."

He looked up at that. "What?"

"For your cabin. I made a list of curtains, rugs, pillows, things like that. Then you need the rods and the pads and hooks and some bookcases. I noticed at your apartment how many books you had that are just stacked haphazardly. You really need some book-cases there and here. That way you could have your books in both places—"

"You're running off at the mouth again. Are you upset?" His eyes narrowed as he studied her.

She shook her head. Not upset, just giddy being around him. Not that she could tell him that. God forbid that he should even guess.

"I fixed lunch. Soup and hot bread." She clamped down on the other words. She would not babble!

"Be there in a sec." He increased the torque.

"Any time. I'll just simmer the soup and keep the bread in the oven. Though it could dry out." Turning abruptly, she headed back to the house.

Jake followed in only moments. While he washed at the sink, she served the meal.

"This is nice," he said as he sat down. "When I come up alone, I usually have sandwiches."

"It's too cold for sandwiches," she murmured, pleased he liked the modest lunch.

"I think the snow is letting up. We could go for a walk later if you wish," he suggested after the first pangs of hunger had been satisfied.

She nodded. "That'd get me out of the house. I don't think I can be getting cabin fever from one morning, but I wouldn't mind going for a walk." She stared into the bowl of soup. Would her life ever get back to normal?

"I called into the station this morning. Nothing new," Jake said as if reading her mind.

She shrugged. "Is that good news? He hasn't broken anything of mine now for a day."

"Two years ago, you were involved pretty heavily with someone who obviously didn't return your feelings. What happened between you two beyond the obvious breakup? Was there anger, bitterness, any reason for retaliation?"

She blinked and met his gaze. Was this the policeman's way of distancing himself from personal involvement? Treat himself and her like third parties, take the personal out of the question?

"No reason for retaliation. No anger that I know of. Mostly bewilderment on my part," she replied slowly. "I mean when things ended, I didn't know what I'd done wrong."

"Surely there was some hurt, some regret, some feeling of wanting to change things, make them come right." He spoke of his own feelings. Funny, until today he had thought he was coping. But the frustration of wanting this woman and not being able to have her threatened to swamp him. Two years ago, he'd made his decision, based on circumstances that appeared to have changed. Yet he didn't think he would make a different decision. Only, he still had regrets.

"So what if there is?" she asked defiantly. If he thought to excuse his behavior or offer some platitude—

"So maybe the man is trying a different tactic, one to make you aware of being alone, of needing him."

She stared at him in horror. Had Jake staged the break-ins just to be the hero riding in to save her? But there had been no need. A phone call and she would have been more than willing to see him again. She had longed for such a call.

No, that didn't make sense. Besides, he'd been with her when her car was broken into. And Jake was too honorable, too much a policeman to ever do anything criminal.

"I don't think I understand what you're talking about," she started. "I didn't walk out of the relationship. You . . . he did."

The phone rang. He leaned over and picked it up. "Morgan." His eyes never left hers.

A tendril of fear snaked up her back. Was this a new report from the Laramie police about something else of hers damaged? Or had they found the man? Was the reason for her staying in Jake's cabin now gone?

"Thanks for the update. We'll be in and out, but keep me informed." He slid the receiver back in place.

"Another break-in?" she asked.

"No. Nothing to report. The information from your neighbor wasn't enough to ID anyone. We know he's a man, but that's all. Too large to be a woman. We know his car is dark, so we're noting any that drive by your place."

Angelica shivered. "I hate this. I feel like I'm the prisoner and I didn't do anything wrong."

"I know it's a strain. But you're holding up well. Most police work is time-consuming. But we'll find him. He'll either make a mistake, or something will turn up to lead us to him. We'll get him."

"I just hope I'm not a basket case before then."

"You're doing fine, honey. There's nothing more I can do for you."

"You could hold me," she blurted out. Her eyes held his, the longing and uncertainty clearly written on her face.

He didn't move; his expression was hard, as if carved from granite.

"Forget it. I—it's just I feel so scared sometimes." He made his feelings obvious. She felt like an idiot asking him to hold her.

"I don't think it's a good idea, Angel."

"Yeah, you're right. I'm a big girl now. I don't need someone to hold me and kiss things better."

Jake closed his eyes momentarily, snapped them open. "It's all right to be afraid. We're going to protect you. We'll find him, I promise."

She nodded, fiddling with the last of her bread. How could she have asked him to hold her? Good grief, she wasn't some baby that needed coddling. She was a mature...

Tears welled in her eyes. She was scared, damn it. Her entire life had been disrupted and she didn't even know why. She just wanted him to hold her.

"Come on, baby." He reached over and lifted her from the chair, leading her into the living room. Sinking down on the sofa, Jake pulled her into his lap and put his arms around her. "This isn't a good idea because of all the lascivious thoughts that race through my mind when you're in my arms," he whispered in her ear. But in contrast to his words, his touch was devoid of passion. His arms held her against his solid chest; his chin rested against her hair. He gently rubbed her back.

Angelica sighed, snuggled closer and relaxed for the first time in days. She closed her eyes and gave herself up to the enjoyment of being held. Jake made everything seem safe. He would find the bad guy and lock him up. She believed him. Things would go back to normal and she'd be safe

Alone, facing the future without the man she loved, but she'd be safe. Thanks to him.

Jake reviewed all his transgressions, trying to see which had been so heinous to warrant this kind of torture. Holding Angelica, just to offer comfort, was hell. He wanted to kiss her, make love to her. Find a spot for her in his world, despite all the odds against them, and keep her for himself. But it wouldn't work. He knew that. And she must know it, too. She never spoke about the time when they were dating. He knew he would not bring it up, either.

Angelica found herself memorizing every second. She drew a deep breath, savoring Jake's special scent. She buried her nose in his chest and held her breath to better remember each different aroma. The smell of his soap, of his after-shave, the laundry detergent used on his shirt, and his own masculine scent that opened the gates to wild, exciting dreams.

She listened to his heartbeat, slow and steady as it pumped the life's blood of the man who was so precious to her. She felt his arms across her back, the hard steel of his thighs beneath her own, the strength of his chest as he cradled her, offering comfort and support. Could she freeze a moment in time? Could she end everything and stay suspended in this minute? She wished it could be. If she lived to be a hundred, she would never forget Jake Morgan. She knew she would love him all her life.

But she also knew life was unfair. She had lost her parents when she was young. She'd missed many things young girls shared with their mothers. And just loving a man didn't mean he'd love in return. Sighing softly, she felt the tears again, but this time they were for what might have been and was not.

"I'm probably crushing you," she whispered, tightening her arms around his neck and bringing her face up to meet his gaze. His lips were mere inches away. She felt his breath fan her cheeks, felt the heat radiating from his body.

"No."

Her smile wobbled. When he cupped her face with his hands and brushed the teardrops from her spiky lashes, her heart melted. He looked worried about her.

"I'll keep you safe, Angel. I won't let him hurt you."

"I'm all right. It's just—I know. I won't worry anymore."

"Oh, I don't know. Maybe you should start worrying—about me." With that, Jake brought his mouth down on hers in a crushing kiss.

Had this really been what she sought? Not comfort, but this bliss? When she was in his arms, she didn't worry or think of the future or regret the past. She only felt. Felt the wonder of his touch, the magic of his embrace, the shimmering sensations that sizzled through her.

She opened her mouth for a deeper kiss and the world spun dizzyingly as he laid her down on the sofa and pressed her into the cushions. Endless moments of spiraling delight whirled around and around as their kiss went on and on. Breathing was forgotten. The blood rushed through her veins, heating every cell, pounding in her ears. Time ceased. Earthly cares hung suspended as they were lost in a world of their own making, one of wonder and passion and love.

When Jake pulled back at last, it was too soon. Angelica gave a small moan of protest, and he kissed her again, then sat up.

"We're moving beyond comfort. Come on, let's take that walk." He rose and went to the window. "It's stopped snowing. It's still overcast, but we won't get wet walking."

Angelica stared at his back in startled surprise. What happened? One moment he was kissing her like there was no tomorrow, the next calmly suggesting they take a walk! Feeling depressed, she sat up and pulled back her hair. There was something wrong when she couldn't keep his attention in the throes of passion. Sighing, she rose on shaky legs and headed for the bedroom.

"I'll be out in a minute," she said as she closed the door behind her. Leaning against it for a long moment, she closed her eyes, reliving the kiss. The kiss of a lifetime, and he wanted to go for a walk in the snow. She shook her head and pushed away from the door. She brushed her hair and quickly braided it to keep it from blowing. Her eyes sparkled back at her in the mirror, her cheeks were bright with color and her lips were rosy. She turned away, her heart heavy.

Jake stood by the door already wearing his shearling jacket. Angelica quickly donned her own jacket and pulled on a knit cap and woolen mittens.

"I'm ready," she said brightly. She would go home tomorrow, no matter what.

Stepping out onto the porch, Angelica caught her breath. The air was so cold it almost snapped. Snow blanketed everything, from the tree limbs bent beneath the weight, to the indistinguishable shape of Jake's car. Smiling in delight at the pristine setting, she boldly stamped down the stairs, making the first marks in the white expanse.

"This is great! We're the first to walk in it."

"Yeah, want to help shovel?" He stood on the porch, watching her, then scanning the area from habit.

"No. And you're not shoveling anything now, either. Come on, you said walk, let's walk."

Bravely Angelica set off, hoping she didn't wind up in some drift. The snow covered her ankles, puffing away from each step as she forged into virgin territory. Two seconds later, Jake joined her, his longer stride eating up the distance.

"Doesn't this remind you of being a kid? We couldn't wait to be finished chores when it snowed so we could play," she reminisced happily. Tilting her head back to look up at him, she waited for his memories. Were they as happy as hers?

He shook his head. "You forget, I'm from Denver. We didn't have expanses of open land like this. I lived in apartments that had parking lots plowed as soon as the first flake fell."

Angelica exhaled, watching the cloud hang suspended in front of her before it gradually dissipated. She eyed the trees ahead of them, then smiled. "So you didn't partake in snowball fights?" she asked innocently.

"Sure, just not often. There weren't a lot of kids around where I lived. Why, you want to fight?"

She shook her head. "Not really. We could make a snowman."

"What about snow angels? I want to see an award-winning angel."

Without any warning, she turned and fell back into the soft snow. Slowly she raised her arms up and down, packing the snow beneath her. She opened and closed her legs.

"For a perfect snow angel, I need help to get up. Otherwise I'll mess the outline," she said, carefully drawing her arms away from the snow and holding out her hands. "Don't step on my skirt!" she warned.

Jake laughed as he reached over and clasped her hands, pulling her upright. Together they studied the outline in the snow.

"Perfect or what?" she asked triumphantly, her heart racing with exhilaration. She enjoyed seeing him laugh. Could she get him to do it again?

"Perfect." Only his eyes were on her, not the outline in the snow.

Angelica was mesmerized by the lights in his dark gaze. "It's all in the technique. And not getting up by yourself. My brothers were too impatient to wait for anyone to help them up. So their angels..." She didn't care what her brothers had done; neither did Jake. She wanted him to kiss her again. Like he had on the sofa. More than comfort, much more.

She almost cried out in denial when he stepped away and continued walking. "I'll remember. It's the technique."

"Like building a snowman," she said, hurrying to catch up.

"That's got a technique to it, as well?" he asked.

"Sure. Kyle always wanted to build the biggest one in the world. So we'd roll the bottom forever, until it was huge. Then the next ball would get too big for us to lift. You have to practice some moderation."

"That was when you were kids. How big do you think we could make one now?"

"Oh, no, not another I-want-to-build-the-biggest-snowman-in-the-world person," she wailed.

"We can at least make one bigger than your brother ever did."

Giving in to the fun, Angelica kept up a running commentary as they rolled the balls to make the snowman. She told Jake about escapades as a child. How her mother worked hard to keep the three children occupied during the long winter days. Chores, activities, quiet time, all came bubbling out in happy reminiscences.

Jake listened, fascinated. He had little to offer in return, but it didn't seem to matter. Angelica had enough stories to keep them entertained all day and night if she chose to keep going.

When it came time to lift the second ball, they worked together, staggering beneath its weight, carefully setting it on the base, packing snow around it to keep it from rolling off. Then the head. Jake lifted it by himself.

"We need a camera," Angelica said when they put the finishing touches on the face. The snowman was as tall as she was. "Kyle will never believe this without a picture. Do you have a camera?"

"No. Just tell him."

"Umm, you don't know Kyle. He has a tendency to believe he knows everything, from what's best for me to how Rafe should expand the ranch. He'll decide I'm just telling a fishing tale and dismiss it." She gave a mock sigh, her eyes dancing. "This is the greatest snowman ever. We'll know it even if we can't convince Kyle."

Jake was curiously silent. His gaze firmly on the snowman, he only nodded absently to Angelica's comments. He was lost in thought.

"Earth to Jake." She shook his arm.

"What?"

"Where were you?"

"Just thinking. Ready to head back?"

"Almost. Let's walk just a little farther."

He missed the gleam in her eye. She kept her face turned a bit lest he guess her plans. Gleeful anticipation rose. She felt like a kid again, carefree and happy.

They walked beyond their creation, the way harder as the snow grew deeper. Soon they were into the trees that lined the open space around Jake's cabin. Angelica paused, leaning over to scrape snow off her boot. Jake continued walking slowly so she could catch up.

Grabbing a handful of snow, Angelica packed it, then tossed it up and caught it. Tossed again, caught it.

Jake turned, eyeing the snowball suspiciously. "We're not having a snowball fight," he stated.

"Stuffy," she replied.

"You'd lose big time, sweetheart." Warily he watched the ball as she tossed it up and caught it again.

"Wanna bet?" she asked softly, stepping closer. Jake took a step back. Angelica advanced another foot. He moved back an equal distance.

Grinning in triumph, she let fly. The snowball hit the heavily laden branch above him and a cloud of snow rained down on Jake, covering him from head to foot.

Laughing aloud, Angelica turned and ran for her life. She'd done this so many times with Rafe and Kyle she knew the routine. If she could only make the cabin, she'd be—

He tackled her from behind, forcing her facedown in the snow. She was laughing too hard to resist. Turning her face to breathe, she couldn't control the giggles. He'd looked stunned as the snow began to slide off the branch.

Rolling her onto her back, he snatched off her hat and grabbed a handful of snow, packing it in around her neck.

"Nooo! That's cold. Stop! Stop!" she shrieked. She tried to escape, but he lay across her legs and held her firmly.

"Damn straight it's cold. Just like the snow down my neck." He reached for another handful of snow but she batted it away, showering them both with the icy powder.

"Okay, I give up. I'm sorry." Her giggles belied the sincerity of her apology.

"Not good enough." He scooped up another handful, threatening.

Angelica knocked it away and reached up to pull him down. Her lips were cold, his cheek colder. She kissed him gently. "I'll gladly grovel, but before the fire, please?"

He captured her cheeks in his cold hands and gazed down at her, his eyes dark and mysterious. She looked lovely. Her face was bright with color, her eyes sparkling, her lips curved in the most delectable smile.

"Angel, you're driving me crazy, do you know that?"

"I'm just trying to have some fun," she said, her smile warm and loving.

Jake rested his forehead against hers, closing his eyes as they lay on the cold ground. Taking a deep breath, he stood, then reached down to pull her upright.

"Cold?" he asked, watching her as she tried to get the snow out of her neckline.

"Just where I'm covered in snow." She couldn't keep from laughing, though. This had been the most fun she'd had in years.

"Me, too. Let's head back. This time, you stay right with me the whole way."

"As close as you'll let me," she murmured, falling into step as he turned toward home.

Jake was careful to keep a couple of feet between them. She didn't know why, but suspected it was to keep his hands to himself. She wished he'd reach out to her. She'd take her mittens off in a second if he'd show any sign of wanting to hold her hand. Instead, he seemed more aloof, more distant than ever. As if they were really the strangers they had become over the past two years. As if the time they'd spent together these past few days had meant nothing. Was she only a case to be solved? Was it only some sense of duty that kept him near?

Jake built up the fire, told Angelica to change into dry clothes, then left to work on the snowmobile. Angelica watched him walk away, a feeling of déjà vu sweeping over her. He'd walked away before, and she hadn't known then that it was goodbye. He was pulling away from her again. They'd enjoyed the afternoon until she'd clearly shown she wanted another kiss. If he'd slammed a door in her face, he couldn't have been any clearer.

"So what is the big deal? You've kissed me before," she said to the empty room. Getting no answer, she headed for the bedroom to change into dry clothes.

Dinner proved to be a strained affair. Neither spoke except to request food to be passed. When Jake said he'd do the dishes, Angelica acquiesced with speed, taking it as a certain indication he didn't want her around.

"I need to get back tomorrow," she said as she carried her plate to the sink.

"No need, you can stay here—"

"It's not a question of my staying here. I have a life to get back to. I appreciate your having me this weekend. And I hope there's been enough time to catch whoever is doing the break-ins. But I have things I need to do. I do have a life apart from being the victim of a crime, you know."

"Hot date to get back to?" he asked sardonically.

"Maybe," she returned, anxious to end this. She longed for her own place.

"Thought you weren't involved with anyone right now." His eyes focused on her as if he could see inside her soul.

She turned and stared him straight in the eye. "That's really not your concern anymore, is it? We dated a couple of years ago, then stopped. Since then, my life, private and public, is my own. It has nothing to do with you."

He paled slightly at her attack, his features still. Only the glittering heat in his eyes gave away his strong feelings.

"You're correct. Your life is no concern of mine. I'll drive you back in the morning. I don't want to chance the roads tonight."

"Tomorrow is fine. Thank you." Head held high, she walked into the bedroom and closed the door with exaggerated care. Methodically she prepared for bed, her mind spinning. She had wanted him to say something, anything, to indicate he cared about her. But he had agreed. She meant nothing. It was past time for her to get on with her life. And Jake would not be a part of it.

CHAPTER SEVEN

"THE bathroom is yours," Angelica said as she came into the kitchen the next morning. She refused to look at Jake, though she could see he wore a shirt this morning. She had packed her bag and set it by the front door. Her coat and hat were on top. She was ready to leave as soon as they finished eating.

Operating on autopilot this morning, she refused to dwell on anything. She had her whole future to think. Today she just wanted to get home.

She went through the motions of cooking oatmeal, setting the table and pouring the coffee as if in a daze. She only had a little longer, then she'd be free. Free of the need to watch every word, every gesture, lest she give herself away. Free of the constant hunger to touch him, listen to him, look at him. Free of the heartache that threatened to drown her.

Hearing the shower, she paused for a moment as she realized sadly their time of playing house was coming to an end. However brief, for the most part it had been fun. She drew out the list she'd made and set it at his place. Whether he followed it or not, she no longer cared. She would not be coming back to the cabin. She would never know if her ideas had worked.

They were silent as Jake drove into Laramie. The highway had been cleared and they made good time. He pulled up before her house and turned off the engine.

"I'll check things out to make sure the place is secure," he said, opening his door.

She nodded, then alighted. Reaching for her bag, she relinquished her key into his hand. It was less trouble to acquiesce than argue. Her chin held high, she led the way up the snowy walk. She'd have to shovel it later. It would give her something to do.

Opening the door, Jake walked in while Angelica stood to one side, waiting. His sweep was brief. He returned and paused beside her. "No sign of any unlawful entry," he said formally.

"Thank you, Officer. I appreciate your help." She stepped inside and pushed the door shut. He caught it before it closed and held it a moment.

"I'll pick you up in the morning and take you to the university. When your car's ready, I'll give you a ride to pick it up."

"That's not necessary, but thank you. I have friends—"

"I'll pick you up in the morning." His hard voice brooked no refusal.

She swallowed. "Very well." Pushing on the door this time shut it. She stood for a long moment, listening as he started his car, turned and drove away.

Fortunately, she had plenty to do. It kept thought at bay. She worked on lesson plans, shoveled the walk and visited briefly with her neighbors. Life had returned to normal.

The next morning, Angelica stood at her front window, watching the street. She and Jake had not set a time when he would come, yet she knew he'd be there early enough for her first class. He was too good a police officer to have let something like her class schedule slip past an investigation. She wondered what else he'd uncovered in trying to solve this case. He couldn't know she didn't date since he kept trying to find out who she was seeing. Why? Did he really suspect someone might be staging these break-ins as retaliation, or was he simply curious?

When his car pulled to a stop in front of her house, she was startled. She'd been so caught up in thought, she'd missed seeing him turn into the street. Putting on her coat, gathering her briefcase, she let herself out of the house. He opened the passenger door for her.

"Good morning."

"Good morning." She could be as formal as he, she thought as she settled in the warm interior. The drive to the university took less than five minutes. He circled Prexy's Pasture and came to a halt before the Ross Building. She glanced at him before opening the door, not meeting his eyes, her gaze on his chin. "Thank you for the ride."

"Your car will be ready at two. I'll pick you up here and take you over."

"I can—"

"Don't argue, Angel. Just do as you're told for once."

"For once! Let me tell you, Jake Morgan, I do as I please, not as some bossy cop tells me."

He ran his fingers through his hair and glared at her. "I didn't sleep worth a damn last night. I've a million things to do. If I take time to come pick you up to take you to get your car, you had better be waiting right here!" He leaned over her, almost shouting in his frustration.

She blinked. "Thank you. I'll be waiting right here at two." She hopped out of the car and slammed the door. Waiting as he accelerated away, she turned, trembling a little in reaction to his harsh tone. Why hadn't he slept last night? And if he were so mad at having to chauffeur her somewhere, why not let someone else do it? She had other friends who would be glad to give her a lift. She needn't depend on him.

Shaking her head, she headed for the steps. Since her office was on the third floor, she liked taking the stairs as a form of exercise. They flanked the end of the U-shaped building. The windows were open in the stairwell, which did nothing to keep the wind out. Each floor had a heavy door that handled that task.

Running up the first flight, Angelica was so busy thinking about Jake she didn't at first see the other person in the stairwell. Suddenly he was in front of her, pushing against her, yanking her briefcase. She staggered, scraped her head against the concrete wall, lost her balance, then fell.

She came to rest in a heap at the bottom of the stairs. Her wrist hurt, her head burned and her ankle throbbed. Gingerly she sat up. Wincing as she pulled some muscles, she shook her head slowly to clear it.

Someone had stolen her briefcase!

Trying to stand, she groaned and sank back to the floor. Her ankle hurt too much to bear any weight.

Hearing some voices near the student union, she called for help. Thankfully it arrived in seconds.

Angelica sat alone in the cubicle at Ivinson Memorial Hospital's emergency room, her legs dangling over the edge of the examination table. She heard Jake's voice. The scrape on her head had been cleaned and treated, her wrist and ankle, both sprained, had been x-rayed and bound. She had answered all the questions the campus police had asked and now awaited someone to take her home. Her department head had been notified and arranged to cover her classes.

She counted the seconds from the time she first heard his voice until he found her. Eight. Pretty good. But then, she had known he was good.

"What the hell happened?" Jake burst into the cubicle like a bull in a raging temper. The waves of frustration and anger radiated from him like steam from a hot spring. His badge was clipped to his coat, his hair wind-tossed and his eyes narrowed and lethal. She shivered, glad she wasn't the focal point of that dangerous energy.

"Someone wanted my briefcase, I guess," she said. "Maybe that's what they wanted all along. Maybe the break-ins will stop now."

"Are you all right?" His voice tempered. He leaned over her, his fingers brushing near the scrape on her forehead. Gently he pushed the hair behind her ear.

"I will be." She swallowed hard, blinking to keep tears away. She longed to reach out for comfort, to have him hold her forever and keep her safe. Taking a shaky breath, she held herself intact.

"Hell, Angel, I said I'd keep you safe and look what happened." The anger was leashed, his voice soft and gentle.

"It's hardly your fault," she said, reaching out to touch his shoulder, the tactile feel of his coat anchoring her. Who was offering comfort to whom? she wondered.

"I should have walked you to your office."

"Oh, come on, Jake, be reasonable. Are you going to shadow me all the livelong day? You delivered me to my office building. No one could predict he'd try something like this. Every other incident has been against my property. He did bump against me, but if I hadn't lost my balance, I might not have fallen. It happened so fast, I couldn't react. By the time I realized what was happening, I was already at the bottom of the steps."

He looked over her, touched her wrist lightly. "Anything broken?"

She shook her head, then winced as it throbbed. "No, just a few scrapes and bruises. And a sprained wrist and ankle. I'll be fine in a few weeks. Really."

"What was in your briefcase?" The switch from concerned friend to official cop was instant.

"Nothing important. Lesson plans. God, I can't believe I have to do some of them over again. This is getting ridiculous."

"There had to be more than lesson plans. Think, Angel."

The curtain to the cubicle slid open and a young resident entered. "Is this your ride home, Professor?" he asked, eyeing Jake suspiciously.

Angelica looked at Jake, her eyebrows raised questioningly.

"Yes, I'm taking her home. Any instructions?" Jake asked.

"We went through them a few minutes ago. She should not be on that foot for the next couple of days. Then she can walk on it as she feels comfortable, providing she wears the support. We've already scheduled a follow-up appointment."

A nurse arrived pushing a wheelchair. Before anyone could move, Jake lifted Angelica and placed her in the chair. "I'll take care of her and see she follows your orders," he said gruffly.

Who says? she wanted to ask, but prudently kept quiet. There would be time to deal with a bossy Jake after they left the hospital.

He drove her home, took her keys and opened her door, then returned to the car and lifted her out.

"I can hop to the house. Put me down. I weigh too much."

"You're not heavy. I think you've lost weight over the past couple of years. You should eat more."

"I eat plenty. Put me down." Her arm encircled his neck, and even through the bulky clothing, she could feel his heat, feel the strength of his chest and arms. She longed to rest her head against his shoulder, longed to give up and let him take care of her, if only for the day.

"In a minute." He walked through the house and directly into the bedroom. Depositing her gently on the bed, he helped her remove her coat and remaining shoe. Drawing a knitted afghan over her, he stood and looked around. He'd seen the room before, of course, when checking out her place. But now he thought about it being her bedroom. A glance at the big bed and he instantly wondered when she had acquired it and why.

A single woman living alone didn't really need a queen-size bed. Had she always been alone? Not liking the trend of his thoughts, he looked at Angelica. She was watching him, a puzzled expression on her face.

"I have to check in at the station, then go home and get a few things. I'll be back in a couple of hours," he said. "Do you need anything before I go?"

"You're coming back? What for? I can get Martha to help me. She won't mind."

"I'm staying here."

"No!"

"Don't argue."

"Jake, you can't stay here. I don't have another bedroom." Her mind was scrambled. There had to be other reasons why he couldn't stay.

"I'll sleep in the living room."

"That sofa is hardly big enough for someone your size."

"I'll manage. Rest until I get back. Do you need anything until then?"

"No, and I don't need you to come back. I have neighbors—"

"Angel, I've already taken the time off. Might as well stay here as at the cabin. If we'd stayed there, this wouldn't have happened."

"I do have a job," she said primly, knowing that wasn't the reason she'd left the cabin.

"What was in your briefcase?"

"You keep asking that."

"I'm trying to find a reason for all this."

"Yeah, I shouldn't forget you're a cop." Shouldn't forget that she had not seen him for over two years. The only reason he was back in her life was because of the recent events. Once he solved the case, would she ever see him again?

"Angel." The hard edge of his voice warned her.

"Okay, okay. Lots of things. I had my attendance book for all my classes, my calendar for the spring semester, an outline of a journal article I'm doing, an invitation to a faculty tea honoring a new professor in the computer science department." She closed her eyes, trying to remember everything that had been in her briefcase. She was so concerned about the lost lesson plans that she had difficulty remembering the other items. "Let me think...the mail I picked up last Thursday from my box but hadn't read. You wouldn't let me take work with me to the cabin, remember? And I didn't get to it yesterday."

He frowned, frustrated. "Why would anyone want any of it? Is the article about some breakthrough?"

"Not really, just a different adaptation on an already much-discussed theorem. It'll get me some brownie points with the higher-ups, but it's certainly not worth stealing. Besides, if anyone used it, we'd know instantly who the culprit was."

"The campus police said you didn't recognize the assailant."

"No, he was tall, taller than I am anyway. He wore a ski mask, a dark blue jacket and dark jeans. It all happened so fast, I didn't notice anything more."

"Angel, you're a bright woman. You must have something someone wants, or wanted, if he got what he was after today. Think about it while I'm gone."

"I don't need you to stay here, Jake," she said once again.

He leaned over and brushed back her hair, cupping her chin with his warm palm. "I need to stay. I need to make sure you are all right." He brushed his lips across her forehead. The touch so light, Angel wondered if she imagined it.

She lay back against the pillows and tried to relax. She was keyed up from both the attack and the thought of Jake staying with her for a day or so. She had wanted to keep her house free of the memories of him, but he'd put paid to that idea. He'd move in, take over and imprint himself on every inch of her home. Sighing in defeat, she closed her eyes. They were linked. Inexorably linked. She couldn't fight fate.

She could only go along for the ride, however long it lasted.

Angelica dozed off and on all day, aware that Jake had returned, conscious that someone else was moving around her place but too lethargic to do anything more than roll over and drift back to sleep.

When she awoke in the late afternoon, she was wide-awake and hungry. Gingerly she sat up, shifting to the edge of the bed until her feet reached the floor. Her ankle throbbed. She considered the distance to the bathroom and hesitated.

Jake appeared in the doorway. "Need help?" he asked, lounging casually against the jamb.

She glanced up, struck again by how tough and dangerous he looked leaning there watching her. In the dim light of the room, he was cloaked in shadows.

"I guess I do. My ankle hurts and I don't think I want to walk on it."

He straightened and walked toward her. "Which is what the doctor said. No walking on it for a couple of days." Without any apparent effort, he scooped her up and headed to the bathroom. He deposited her inside and stepped out. "Call when you're finished," he said just before the door clicked shut.

Jake had prepared dinner. Carrying Angelica into the living room and depositing her gently on the sofa, he mentioned it would be ready soon. Soft music played from her stereo, the curtains had been drawn against the darkness and the lamps gave a warm glow to the room. She wished again she had a fireplace. The evenings they'd spent before his at the cabin had been wonderful.

Most of the time she spent with Jake was wonderful.

"This is delicious," Angelica said a few moments later when she tasted his chicken casserole.

"Thanks. It's easy."

"Somehow I didn't picture you cooking much," she murmured. Plenty of men cooked. Her brothers were excellent cooks, though neither particularly liked to cook. But she had not pictured Jake cooking.

"I have to eat. Did you think I ate every meal out somewhere?" he replied, sitting opposite her with his own plate.

She shrugged. She hadn't thought it through. They'd eaten out a lot when dating. She'd cooked the meals at the cabin.

"Where did you learn to cook?" she asked.

"At home. When I was a kid, my uncle didn't get home until late, so I usually started dinner. Cooked the entire meal most nights."

"You lived with your uncle?" She'd known he was an only child. When she had asked him about his parents once long ago, he'd merely mentioned they were dead.

"From the time I was six until I went to college."

"Just the two of you?" she asked.

"Yes. He never married."

She looked at him, wondering about a lot of things. He never talked about his past. They had been too caught up in the present two years ago, and that had lasted only a few months. Only long enough for her to fall in love. What had his childhood been like?

"Tell me about growing up with your uncle."

He looked at her and shrugged. "What's to tell? We shared an apartment. I learned to cook."

"Do you see much of him now?"

He shook his head. "He died when I was in college."

"Longevity does not seem to run in your family," she commented.

He smiled wryly. "They were all accidents. My folks were killed in an airplane crash. My uncle was a cop, but he didn't die on duty. He was killed when he fell from a tall ladder, trying to help a friend put up storm windows."

"Was he the reason you became a cop?"

"Yeah."

"So you don't have any family?"

He shook his head once, his eyes narrowed as if he was trying to guess what she was leading up to.

"I lost my parents, but I always had Rafe and Kyle. Now I have Charity and little Christopher, too."

"Rafe's wife and son?" he clarified.

She nodded, smiling. "That's their latest family picture, on the second shelf. Isn't he the sweetest baby? You'd think Rafe invented fatherhood the way he's so crazy for his son. Almost as crazy as he is about Charity," she said wistfully. She envied her older brother the love he'd found. He and his wife didn't mind everyone in the world knowing how much they loved each other. She wished she had the same kind of love. Wished Jake loved her as much as she loved him.

"So your grand love affair didn't pan out," he said softly.

She blinked, hurt he'd mock her. He didn't need to rub her nose in the fact he couldn't love her. And he needn't be cruel about it, either. With dignity, she raised her chin. "I guess not. I'm not ashamed of feeling the way I do."

"I'm sorry, Angel."

She knew he meant it. He wasn't a cruel man, just one who didn't love her. She nodded, toying with the last bit on her plate. Restlessly, she shoved it aside and put the plate on the end table. "Thank you for dinner. It was delicious."

"Coffee?" Jake rose and gathered the plates, heading for the kitchen.

"Yes. There's some brandy over the refrigerator. I want some of that, too." A timeless remedy for aches and pains of all kinds.

He brought their mugs filled with fragrant coffee and the hint of brandy. Handing her one, he sat beside her on the sofa, resting his arm across the back, his fingers touching her hair.

"If I could change things for you, I would, Angel," he said in a low voice, dropping his hand to her shoulder, pulling her closer until she lay snuggled against his side.

"But just wishing it so won't make it so," she replied sadly.

"No, you can't make people love you no matter how much you might want to." He'd learned that himself the hard way.

Angelica took a sip of hot coffee. It burned all the way down, which jolted her out of the maudlin mood she was fast sinking into.

"So, did anything turn up today while I slept?" she asked, determined to keep the tears at bay, at least until she was alone in her room.

"Nothing about the perpetrator. No one saw him but you. However, your briefcase turned up in a trash can behind the geology building. Empty."

"At least that wasn't lost. It was a gift to me from my brothers when I got my Ph.D. I'll be glad to have it back."

"We've pretty much eliminated the air force angle. Most of the people we've talked to didn't even know you did work for them."

"Honestly, are you telling that to everyone I know?" she asked.

"We're questioning people who might have some leads for us."

"The work at the air force is supposed to be kept secret. I didn't tell people because of that requirement."

"Most of the people we've interviewed were impressed by that facet of your professional life. They aren't going to try to pick your brain."

"So if it's not related to that work, you think it's connected to the university?"

"Unless you have some top-secret formula for fattening cattle that some ranching syndicate is trying to get."

She chuckled. "No. I leave that to Kyle and Rafe. I go home to help out sometimes, but I'm not passionately in love with ranching like those two. Ever been on a cattle ranch?"

"Nope. I believe I like thinking that beef comes in neat little packages in the supermarket, rather than covered in hide and mooing."

"A realist, I see." She would like to invite him to the ranch. Even if he knew nothing about cattle and horses, she'd bet he'd fit right in. There was something about men like him and her brothers and the ranch hands on Rafter C that spoke of confidence and assurance. They knew who they were, what they were capable of. Even the arrogance was similar. She smiled, wondering how he would react meeting one of her brothers.

Taking a sip of her coffee, she savored the warmth. It had cooled enough to be consumed without burning. The brandy slid down smoothly. Soon the ache in her ankle and wrist would fade. Maybe even the ache in her heart.

"I see what you mean about no fireplace. Wish we were back at the cabin," Jake murmured, shifting a bit lower on the sofa, resting his legs beside hers on the coffee table. He settled Angelica into a more comfortable position, so she was leaning half on him, half against the sofa.

"Are you going to buy the things I suggested?" she asked, curious.

"Sure, if you go with me. I don't know what to buy."

"I was very clear." She would not go shopping with him. The time for playing house had ended.

"Then what did you mean by pictures?"

"Pictures, you know, images captured to be put on a wall."

He glanced around her room, noting the soft Monet reproductions, the photographs that were displayed everywhere. Then he looked down at her. "You choose," he said softly. "Something that will remind me of this place. It's nice, relaxing, pretty. Like you." Lowering his head, he kissed her. He tasted of coffee and brandy and male heat. Angelica sighed and gave herself up to the delight of being in his arms. She moved her lips against his, savoring every second.

He took the cup from her numb fingers and placed it beside his on the table. Turning her, he dragged her across his chest, kissing her again and again, his hands threading through her silky hair, rubbing the length of her spine, moving to cup one breast.

Her breath caught, her heart pounded. She moved closer, wanting to become a part of him, wanting nothing to separate them ever. When his tongue slipped between her lips, she met him with her own. Her hands clutched his broad shoulders, the sting in her wrist unnoticed because of the overwhelming sensations that shimmered through her.

He kissed her over and over, as if she were life-giving water and he a dying man in the desert. His hands caressed and fondled, brushed and petted. She was burning up with longings and burgeoning desire. Her senses were intoxicated and all reality was suspended as she floated on a cloud of rapture.

She wanted more, much more. She would have willingly given anything he asked. But all he wanted were kisses. Mind-drugging kisses. Kisses that brought a greater high than anything else she'd ever known.

Damn it, damn it, damn it. Why couldn't he love her? She was so crazy about the man she thought she would go insane, and he was sorry he couldn't love her.

But he could kiss her enough that she knew nothing else would ever satisfy her again. Kiss her enough that she knew she'd long for similar embraces all her life. Nothing would ever measure up. And it wasn't fair. If he didn't want her, he should not be spoiling her for every other man in the world. She would never be satisfied with anyone else. She wanted Jake Morgan.

CHAPTER EIGHT

THE phone rang, waking Angelica. She reached for it, almost dropping it in her haste. "Hello?"

"How are you feeling this morning?" Jake's familiar voice came through loud and clear.

She blinked and sat up. Glancing around in bewilderment, she realized she was in bed, in her nightgown, and the sun was shining brightly.

"What time is it?" she asked, still feeling groggy.

"It's after ten. I thought you would be up by now. Did I wake you?"

"Yes, but it's okay. It's too late to sleep. Where are you?" She would not think about last night. Her fingers pressed against her lips. They were slightly swollen. Smiling, she remembered the kisses. No! She wasn't going to think about that right now.

"I'm at the station. I'm going by the university in a little while to get a list of all your students. Then you and I are going over them one by one to see who might have any kind of reason for these acts against you."

"Last semester's classes?"

"Last semester's, the one before and this term's. Can you manage by yourself until I get there?"

"Of course. I feel much better today. Tomorrow I need to get back to class. I can't expect others to cover for me when all that's hurting is an ankle. I can sit to lecture."

"We'll see."

"No, we—" He hung up before she could make it perfectly clear to the man that she knew how to run her own life. If she wanted to teach tomorrow, she'd do it. There was an elevator to the third floor where her office was. She could manage that. And there was a ramp into the building where she taught. Worst case, she'd rent a wheelchair and find a student to push her.

Student. Jake obviously thought it might be one of her students. But why? What did she have that they wanted?

Angelica was dressed and in the living room when Jake arrived shortly after noon. Martha Benson had been by, bringing lunch and a cane she'd had to assist Angelica in becoming more mobile. Because of her wrist, she couldn't use crutches, but the cane helped immensely.

She met Jake at the door, proud to be on her own two feet.

He took in the situation with a quick glance, then leaned over to kiss her, sweeping her up in his arms before she could protest. The cane clattered to the floor as her arms flew around him to hold on.

"The doctor told you to stay off that foot for two days. Is this how you mind?" he said as he strode into the kitchen and sat her down in a chair. He pulled out a second one and propped her foot carefully on it.

"I'm not a child," she grumbled. She'd been so proud of getting around and he was acting as if she'd committed a crime.

"You're acting like one. Is that lunch?" He nodded to the plate piled high with freshly made sandwiches, and a covered bowl beside it.

"Yes, Martha brought it over. She, er, knew I had company staying with me, so made enough for an army. I guess she took one look at your size and figured you needed plenty to keep going."

"You eat half. You're too skinny." He took off his coat and hooked it over the back of a chair. After getting plates from the shelves, he sat opposite her.

"I eat plenty."

"You've lost weight in the past two years. Were you pining away for love?" he asked sardonically.

"You've a mean streak in you," she said, yanking her plate in front of her and reaching for a roast beef sandwich. "Just because you don't believe in love, doesn't mean others don't."

"You're too smart and have too much going for you to waste away for love."

"You've got that right. I'm going ahead with my life!"

He sat back in his chair, watching her, amusement dancing in his eyes. "How are you going to do that?"

Haughtily she lifted her eyebrow. "I don't believe that is any concern of yours. You made that perfectly clear. Did you bring home the class listings?"

"Yes." He leaned over, reached inside his jacket and withdrew a computer printout. Unfolding it, he spread it out on the table.

"Good grief, I never had that many students."

"These are for all your classes last year and the year before, as well as the current semester."

"I wouldn't count the current students. The first break-in happened over the Christmas break. Why would one of those students want to break in?"

"Why would any of them want to?" He shoved the list across to her. "Tell me what you know about each one."

She scanned the list for the first class. "You know, Jake, we can narrow this down right away by eliminating the women and short men. I mean, the guy on the steps was taller than me, so that would eliminate anyone under five-nine. And we know it was a man."

"Good, cross them off." He tossed her a pen.

Nibbling on her sandwich, Angelica read through the list, pausing now and then as she had to search her memory to bring an image to mind. She quickly crossed off the women and a few of the men. Rereading the list, she had to think about some of them. Finally she was finished.

"Here." She was surprised to find she'd finished her sandwich and eaten some of the salad Martha had sent. "Want to make some coffee?"

"Sure." He moved easily around her kitchen as if he'd been there forever. He had no trouble locating the coffee, the mugs. He leaned against the counter, watching her as the coffee brewed. "Did anything come to mind as you marked the list?"

"Nothing that would tie in with what's been happening. I can't think of a reason for any of these kids to want to break into my house or car. Office, maybe, if it were finals time. But it all happened after finals. I don't think it's a student."

He shrugged. "It may not be."

"Jake..." Angelica dropped her gaze to her plate, her finger tracing a pattern on the edge. "I was invited to a reception for the new computer science professor. It's Saturday night. Would you go with me?" She held her breath. The seconds ticked by with agonized slowness. Finally she dared risk a peek into his face.

He was all hard angles and planes. His eyes were dark and fathomless, his expression remote. "Why?"

"I'd like you to," she said.

He turned to pour the coffee. "If we haven't found the man by then, I'll go. I don't want you going anywhere by yourself."

Feeling deflated, she sighed softly. At every opportunity, he hammered at her the fact he was only with her because of the problems in her life. Once they caught the man, she'd never see him again. Or only at a distance, maybe, in passing.

"Is it fancy?" he asked, sliding her mug before her.

"A bit. A suit is all."

"I won't have anything to say at a gathering of university professors," he warned.

She smiled. "I wouldn't worry about that if I were you. You won't have to say anything to the women. They'll fall all over themselves just to stand near you. You'll be hotter than Costner. And the men will be so anxious to prove to you that they are just as masculine, they'll be the ones anxious to please."

A dull flush spread on his cheeks and his eyes grew even darker.

Angelica was charmed at the reaction to her teasing. Not wanting to push her luck, however, she refrained from expanding on it. "You'll have to drive. You can pick me up in time to be there at seven."

"I'll still be here," he said easily.

"I don't need a baby-sitter."

"I'm staying. I'd offer to have you at my place, but this is nicer. You ready for a nap?"

"No, I don't want a nap. And I'm not going in the bedroom to lie down, so don't even suggest it. I spent almost all day yesterday there. I only sprained my ankle. I'm not an invalid," she snapped. The stress was beginning to get to her.

"Then we can go over the list."

"I don't want to do that, either. I don't know why anyone would be bothering me. None of these kids has any reason that I can think of. I don't need to go over each one."

"Are you often this crabby?" he asked mildly.

She glared at him. "You're the reason I am. Why don't you go away and leave me alone?"

Jake stood, put his mug on the counter and snagged his jacket. Angelica's heart dropped. She didn't really want him to go, though she knew it was the best thing. Damn it, she wanted him to stay with her and grow to love her.

"I'll be back," he said and left.

She banged her fist on the table. He'd only done as she'd asked, so why was the anger and frustration so strong?

Hopping, she cleared her place and hobbled into the front room. She carefully leaned over to pick up the cane that rested where she'd dropped it. Using it, she got a book and sank gratefully onto the sofa. She'd read. She was in no mood to work, or call anyone, or sleep. She was in no mood for anything.

She heard the key in the lock some time later and looked up. She had only read three pages in the past half hour. Her thoughts spun around Jake.

He walked in, bringing the fresh cold air from outside. The sunlight seemed brighter. For no reason, Angelica felt better.

He glanced at her, then headed for the bedroom. In only a moment, he was back with a pair of thick woolen socks. He tossed them to her.

"Put them on. I'll get your coat. We're going out."

"Where?" Intrigued, she sat up and drew on the socks.

He returned with her jacket and knit cap. "Shopping. I rented a wheelchair so you'll be mobile."

"I don't want—"

"Just shut up and get ready. You're going to help me buy the things on the list for the cabin."

A bubble of anticipation rose. She hadn't meant to become so involved that she ended up shopping with him, but it beat staying in the house. And she could make sure he got exactly what she'd envisioned. Make sure he had the items to make his cabin the comfortable home he wanted. She could do that for him if nothing else.

In no time they were on I-80 heading for Cheyenne.

"We could have shopped in town," she said.

"The mall in Cheyenne will be better for the wheelchair. And it won't be so cold."

"I could walk. The cane was enough support."

"No, the doc said to stay off the foot for two days. The chair will do."

"This is nice of you to go to all this trouble to entertain me. What can I do to pay you back?" Angelica asked.

"Do what you're told for a change," he replied.

"Of course, as long as what I'm told is what I want to do. But I promise to be totally agreeable on this jaunt."

"That will be a switch."

"Not so, Jake. I can be very agreeable. Just you watch."

He glanced over to her, noting her smug smile as she gazed out the windshield. She was always easy to be with, even when she was in a snit. He smiled slightly, wondering what her idea of being totally agreeable was. How far could he push her? It would be an interesting day.

Angelica teased and flirted and enjoyed herself tremendously. From the first moment when they arrived in the mall, she set upon her task to make the shopping venture memorable. She knew from her brothers that men did not like shopping. Her goal was to make sure Jake remembered this trip all his life.

Jake initially protested every suggestion she made. At first, Angelica was fighting mad, but by the third time, she realized he was teasing her in return. From then on, they grew more and more outrageous in their discussions about the curtains, rugs and other accessories for the cabin. The poor saleswoman was bewildered and tried to be so diplomatic. Twice, Angelica caught Jake's eye and they exchanged a secret smile at the obvious efforts of the saleswoman. In the end, they bought nearly everything on the list.

Giggling softly as he pushed the chair out into the open part of the mall, Angelica waited until they'd left the store before turning around to look at him. "We were awful. That poor woman."

He matched her grin. "She got a hefty commission out of the final sale. She'll be fine. What were you doing arguing with me? I thought you were going to be totally agreeable."

"Jake, I was being reasonable. That purple rug you wanted for the bathroom was atrocious!"

"It's my bathroom. Want to stop for a cup of coffee?" He paused by a bakery that had small tables scattered around.

Taking a deep breath, Angelica nodded. When their order had been placed, she picked up the gauntlet. "It's your bathroom, but others will be using it."

He leaned back in his chair, all casual male animal. His long legs stretched out before him, he regarded her with a lazy, possessive air. "You're pretty when you get worked up about something," he said unexpectedly.

Angelica's breath caught in her throat. Her eyes widened and she stared at him, caught up in his own male beauty. He carried himself with such a don't-give-a-damn attitude, he was almost scary. But she never feared him, only her own reactions and feelings around him. Now watching him stare at her caused her heart to race. She wanted to fling herself into his lap and hold on for dear life. The image of their kisses the other night sprang into her mind. Unconsciously she licked her lips. His gaze was drawn to her mouth and slowly he sat up, reached over and brushed her damp lips with the pad of his thumb. Cupping her chin with his palm, he rubbed her lips again.

Angelica felt the touch to her toes. Every cell quivered to attention. Butterflies danced in her stomach. Her eyes were captured by his and she couldn't look away. She knew he'd see the love residing deep within her, but there was nothing she could do to conceal that. He already knew, so what did it matter? He knew and it changed nothing.

"You're dangerous to be around." His voice was so low she had to strain to hear.

"Why?" A whisper only, but she hadn't the strength to speak aloud. Bonded to Jake by the touch of his hand, by the caress of his thumb, she clutched the arms of the wheelchair tightly to keep herself from throwing her arms around his neck. They were in a public place, for heaven's sake. She had to demonstrate a modicum of decorum.

"Because you get a man thinking things he has no business thinking. Wishing for things that aren't possible." He released her and sat back, breaking eye contact as he scanned the bakery, looking for their waitress. Spotting her walking toward them, he kept his eyes on her.

Angelica couldn't look away. What had he meant?

"Here you go, folks. A chocolate éclair, a brownie and two cups of coffee." Placing the order on the table, the waitress smiled and turned away.

Angelica didn't want the sweet. She wanted to go home. She wanted them to be alone, where she could climb into his lap and make him kiss her as if there was no tomorrow.

"Change your mind?" he asked as she continued to stare at him, ignoring the éclair.

"Let's go home," she said, her voice husky with emotion.

His eyes locked on hers. Long moments slowly passed.

"No," he said briefly.

She broke contact and reached for her fork. The éclair tasted like chalk. But she ate every bit of it. The coffee warmed her. She hadn't realized how chilled she'd grown. Finally finished, she idly glanced around the bakery. The brightness of the day had faded. She was getting tired. Maybe she should go home and take a nap.

"Tomorrow I'm going to work," she said, not looking at him.

"If you feel up to it."

"I do. But I'm tired now. We've gotten most of the things on the list. Can we go home? I want to take a nap."

She remembered from before that sleep helped when she was depressed. It afforded an escape and for the moment was what she wanted most.

"I still need to get the pictures."

"Another time, Jake. I'm tired." She refused to meet his eyes.

Angelica went straight to bed when she reached home. She slept until dinner, ate, then returned to her room. Reading, she tried to quell all thoughts of Jake until she finally fell asleep.

The next morning, she dressed and was ready to leave for the campus in time for her first class. She didn't speak as he drove her. The wheelchair had been returned and she was relying on the cane. Her ankle was better today, and her wrist barely pained her.

"I'll walk you to class," he said, pulling the car to a halt before the Ross Building.

"Thank you." She didn't want to admit she was just a bit nervous. Not that she was carrying anything anyone would want today, only her shoulder bag. Still, it would take a while for the uncertainty to fade.

Jake not only walked her to her room, he sat in the back during the class, studying the students, watching Angelica.

"You didn't have to wait," she said after the last student had left at the end of the hour.

"I only had a couple of math courses in college. My major was criminology. But if I'd taken one of yours, I might have signed up for more. You make it sound so exciting, as if it's the greatest subject in the world," he said, ignoring her comment.

"I like it," she said stiffly.

"It shows. And you make it come alive for these kids. I loved your example about the cattle ranch."

"So much of math is practical, but people don't always realize it."

"So you make sure they do."

She nodded, pleased he liked her teaching technique.

"I shouldn't be surprised. You bring a lot of enthusiasm to everything you do," he said thoughtfully.

"For the most part, life is wild and wonderful. Why not express it?"

"Yeah, why not? Where to next?"

"I have a break for an hour, then another class. You really don't have to hang around."

"I want to," he said simply.

Jake stayed with her all day Wednesday and Thursday. Friday was a free day, and she had him drop her off at her office and then leave. She needed to get caught up on all the administrative work involved with her job as well as redo the lost lesson plans. And she needed to do it alone. He was too distracting.

Saturday he was gone most of the day. She longed to ask about his plans but refrained. It smacked too much of involvement and she was trying to break away. Besides, she wanted to take a nap and elevate her foot to be in shape for the reception that evening.

By six-thirty she was ready. She had curled her hair
and arranged it on top of her head, letting long ten-
drils cascade down in the back. The dress she chose
was a warm, light woolen one, pale cream with a blue
pattern that caught the color of her eyes. She had no
choice of footwear, only a flat shoe for her right foot
and a warm sock to cover the bulky support on her
injured left foot. Walking through a cloud of perfume
spray, she was ready.

She had not heard from Jake all day and hoped he
remembered he'd agreed to take her to this event. It
would be similar to previous ones she'd attended.
Except for the first time in over two years, she had
an escort. And what an escort. Preening in feminine
pride, she knew she'd be with the best-looking man
there.

He used his key to open the door. She hobbled out
into the hall and stopped. He looked gorgeous. The
dark charcoal gray suit enhanced his dark good looks,
made him look even more dangerous than usual.

"Wow," she said softly,

He frowned. "Court suit. You ready?"

She smiled and walked forward until she was almost
touching him. Tilting back her head to see, she nodded
slowly. "I think we should give it a miss, though."

"Why?"

"Because one look at you and everyone will forget
the guest of honor."

"Right." He leaned over and kissed her lightly on
the lips. Pulling back, he opened his eyes and stared
down into hers. "I'll give it a miss if you want." His
voice poured through her like hot wine. She took a
deep breath, smelling Jake's heady scent. For a
moment, she gave serious thought to staying home,

to pulling him into her bedroom and shutting the door behind them.

But much as she was tempted, she couldn't do it. She wanted more when she gave herself. A one-night stand wasn't for her or Jake.

She cleared her throat. "I need to go. It's good form, you know. And when I make professor, I want everyone to come to my party." Reluctantly she broke away and looked around for her coat. She was having trouble focusing.

"Invite me when that event occurs. I'll come," he said, reaching into the closet and drawing out her heavy coat. He fastened it, ending with the button beneath her chin. Cupping her chin, he raised her face for another kiss, his lips covering hers in a warm embrace.

Angelica really didn't want to go.

The reception was in full swing when they arrived. Jake had his arm around her waist, half-holding her to minimize the weight on her ankle.

"Find a chair and sit. I'll get you a drink," he said, scanning the room.

"Will you stop that? Every time we go anywhere, you check the place out as if you're expecting a gang of terrorists. It's creepy."

"It's also the best way to avoid trouble. Be prepared for it. Where do you want me to put you?"

"Like I was a sack of apples. Over there, by Professor Holcome. At least he's entertaining to talk to. Once you drop me, I'll probably not see you again until it's time to go home."

"Don't bet on it, sweetheart."

To Angelica's surprise, Jake returned with a drink for each of them. He sat on the arm of her chair and gave no indication he wanted to move an inch.

She wondered once or twice if he'd be bored with the conversation. It tended so often to gravitate toward university concerns. Probably cops talk shop when they got together, too.

"... two errors, which I quickly corrected. Computers are fine, but only as accurate as the person entering the data," Gerald Holcome was saying.

"Sorry, I missed the first part," Angelica said. She had to pay attention.

"I said I compared the computer-generated grade sheet with my own records and found two errors. Not that one student would have minded. His score and the other's were reversed. It pays to double-check. Don't you do so, Angelica?"

"Yes, I do, actually. But I've never found an error. Did the grades from last semester come out?"

"They were in the mail last week, Wednesday or Thursday, I think. I know I did my checking over the weekend."

Angelica gave Jake a telling glance. "I didn't get to read my Thursday mail. My briefcase was stolen with the mail in it."

"I heard. Sorry about all that. Tell administration. They can get you a duplicate."

"Actually, I don't have my notes, either. My office was broken into and trashed. When I got everything squared away, my lesson plans, sample final exams and grades were missing. I didn't worry about it too much because I'd already turned in my grades."

Jake leaned over. "Tell me about the grading system. You send in the grades, the administration department keys them into a computer, then sends you a listing to verify accuracy?''

Professor Holcome nodded. "That's right. The grades have already been posted, but it never hurts to double-check. If there are errors, we can catch them. As I did with these two young men.''

"Angel, were you missing the grades for your fall classes?''

She nodded. "And the ones for last spring, too. But it didn't matter since I had already turned in my grades.''

"Could they be changed?''

"I don't see how.''

"Hackers can get into any computer. Could someone have changed grades in the university computer? Someone who then made sure you could never double-check the listing?''

"It's possible," Gerald Holcome said before Angelica could answer. She nodded in agreement. It was possible.

"Tomorrow we get a copy of the grades and you see which ones you remember. If any are glaringly different, we'll have a starting point.''

"Good grief, Jake. I had over a hundred and fifty students. I can't remember what grade each one earned.''

"It's worth looking at.''

"I say, is this detective work?'' Professor Holcome asked excitedly.

Angelica turned back to Gerald, exasperated. "Yes. Get the famous detective to tell you some of his other exploits. I wanted to enjoy the party, not think about this. Apparently policemen never leave their work.''

"One of the hazards of the job," Jake murmured, his hand curling around her bare neck. Gently his warm fingers rubbed her skin, sending waves of electricity shivering through her.

Angelica leaned against him, her shoulder against his hip. "You're off duty tonight, Officer. Enjoy yourself."

"I am." His thumb brushed the lobe of her left ear, rubbed the sensitive skin behind it. It was all Angelica could do to remain in her chair. She was going to get him for this. And get him good. How dare he practically make love to her before the professor! And in a room full of people!

CHAPTER NINE

"I ALWAYS wanted to be a detective. I remember once when I was a young man..."

Angelica tuned out Gerald's ramblings and let her gaze drift around the room, but she couldn't concentrate on anything but Jake. Blast! She wished to give the appearance of being totally oblivious to him. If he guessed how he affected her, would he stop touching her or would his attentions escalate?

And why did he bother? He'd made it clear more than once that he wasn't interested. At least not interested in what she wanted. Yet he continued to touch her, caress her, kiss her. Heat washed into her cheeks and warmed her. How he kept kissing her— X-rated and wild! Dangerous too, because it was hard to stop with only kisses. Now his fingers seemed to have developed a will of their own. How could he calmly converse with the professor when his touch set off drumrolls and clashing cymbals inside her? She knew her heartbeat was loud enough to be heard across the room. Wasn't he affected at all?

She was grateful when Susan Standford joined them. At least Jake stood then and offered his hand, breaking contact, giving Angelica breathing room.

"I'm so pleased to meet you, Detective. We all wondered who Angelica brought with her. She usually comes to these things alone. But when I heard you were the one investigating the assault, well, I just had to come meet you and tell you we would all do any-

thing to help.'' Susan was of average height, yet next
to Jake she looked almost petite. Her dark hair was
cut short, her brown eyes were deep and sultry as she
flirted provocatively.

Angelica gritted her teeth. ''Your mistake, Susan.
Jake is not handling the investigation. He and I are
longtime friends.''

Jake glanced at her, his expression carefully neutral.
Thoughtfully he nodded and turned back to Susan.
''Angel and I go back quite a while. Do you teach in
the mathematics department, as well?''

''Oh, no, I'm in anthro.'' Susan smiled flirtatiously
and then looked at Angelica. ''You don't mind if I
take Jake and introduce him to everyone? I know
you're fairly immobile with that ankle. We'll be right
back.'' Tucking her hand into his arm, she drew him
across the room. Angelica was not so pleased with
Susan after all. Not that she betrayed her emotions
by even a flicker of her eyelids. She had no hold over
Jake. For a moment, she watched to see how he would
make out, meeting so many men and women from
the university crowd. The two life-styles were so different. Would he feel out of place?

Slowly Angelica stood, leaning on the cane Martha
had lent her. ''Gerald, I'd like to mingle a bit. Would
you walk around with me?'' She refused to watch Jake
any longer. He was a grown man and he could fend
for himself. And she needed to fend for herself.
Angelica congratulated Professor Sorenson on his
promotion and visited with several friends. She
answered endless questions about her fall and the
break-in of her office. She did not expand on the situation by letting anyone know about her house and

car. Speculation and gossip were rampant without that.

It was clear everyone else thought, as Susan Standford had, that Jake was accompanying her for protection, and that he was investigating the case. As she sipped a glass of white wine, she looked over to him. It was an obvious conclusion. He was a policeman and she had not brought another man to any university affairs in over two years. When they'd been dating, she had been reluctant to share him with anyone. And then once he'd stopped calling, she had not wanted to spend her time with other men. Sighing, she wondered if tonight had been a mistake. Would she forever be questioned about her longtime friend whom no one had known?

She put down her glass and limped slowly across the reception hall. Stopping beside Jake, she smiled at the group of men and women who were discussing the latest Costner film. He glanced down, smiled and slipped his arm around her waist. Gratefully, Angelica leaned against him.

When she was asked about the film, she had to reply, "I haven't seen it yet." She rarely went to the movies. She didn't like going alone. Given the way gossip spread through the university, she didn't want to become the latest topic of discussion for all the college students. Better to rent a video.

"We could go tomorrow," Jake murmured softly.

"I thought you'd seen it," she said, warmed by the offhand invitation.

"Wouldn't mind seeing it again. Then I could see if Jason's assessment of the hidden social implications is accurate."

"It is, Jake. Would I lead anyone astray?" The young assistant professor of sociology grinned engagingly.

"Put it down to my suspicious nature. Cops like to investigate things on their own," Jake responded. He looked at Angelica again. "We've got to be going. It's been a pleasure." He eased her away from the group and toward the door.

"Do you have a late date?" she asked, walking beside him, leaning on him a bit more than earlier. Her ankle hurt, her arm ached and her head had begun to pound.

"No. You do, with a bed. You look exhausted." He got her coat, slipped it on her and tilted up her face. "Have you visited enough?"

"Yes. But I don't need you watching over me—"

"You need someone, or you'll stay all night and put back your recovery by a week."

"Thank you, *Dr. Morgan*, for your expert medical assessment of the situation."

"Mouthy." He brushed his lips over hers, which effectively shut her up.

Shut her up and left her reeling. Angelica wanted to look around to see who might have noticed, but she dared not. Better to ignore the gesture and leave with some dignity. She hoped everyone in the room was too busy with their own conversations to notice Jake's kiss.

In less than ten minutes, Jake pulled his car up in front of Angelica's town house. When he opened her door, he did not give her the chance to step out, but reached in and scooped her up.

"Jake! I can walk. Put me down."

"You're tired. It's a short way to the house." By the time he finished talking, he'd reached her front stoop. Setting her gently on her feet, he waited as she found her key. Taking it from her cold fingers, he inserted it and opened the door. Gently he urged her inside and closed the door behind them. "Thank you for asking me to go with you tonight, Angel. I enjoyed meeting the people you work with on a social level."

"Still think one of them is trying to steal my article idea?" she asked, shrugging out of her coat. She steadied herself against the wall. She was more tired than she realized.

"No. But talking with Gerald has given me another lead to check out. First thing Monday, I'm going to get a list of all your students' grades from last semester and we're going over them to see if any have been altered."

"Like I'm going to remember exactly what each student earned," she complained. Couldn't he have waited to tell her that? Couldn't he have pretended at least that tonight had been social rather than business?

"It's a starting place. Do you need any help getting to bed?"

She shook her head.

"I'll pick you up tomorrow around three."

"Why?"

"For the show."

"Oh, you don't really have to take me. I can wait for it to come out on video."

"We made a date. I have witnesses," he said whimsically.

She smiled. "So you do. Fine, I'll be ready at three."

He reached out and drew her into his arms. Angelica gave a sigh and raised her face. Suddenly her zipper slid down, the cool air startling against her skin.

"Jake!"

"Relax, Angel. I'm just helping. This looked awkward to unfasten with your wrist." He released the fasteners of her bra.

Daring images danced in her mind. She could see herself slipping her arms from the dress, letting it trail down her body as Jake watched. Desire flooded her. She wanted him. She had loved him for so long, yet had been denied his presence in her life for two years. Slowly she raised her face to his, letting that love shine from her eyes.

"God, Angel, look at me like that and I won't be responsible for what I might do."

Slowly she parted her lips. "Maybe I don't care," she said huskily. Stepping closer, she reached up to encircle his neck. The cool air on her back contrasted with the burning heat wherever she touched Jake. She felt his warm hands on her bare skin and smiled in delight. She felt feminine, soft and dainty. Angling her mouth, she captured his lips and tightened her hold.

A muffled groan escaped Jake as he clamped her so tightly against him she couldn't breathe. Not that she wanted to. She feasted on the embrace as if it was ambrosia. His taste was achingly familiar, disturbing, exciting. The solid strength of his body dominated hers, giving her a precious sense of safety and security. The flames licking throughout her contrasted to that security. They were dangerous, daring and demanding. She wanted more. More of Jake, more of the love that she felt so strongly.

Slowly the embrace changed. The heat between them raged hot and strong, but Jake eased back, his eyes opening to gaze down into hers. To drown in the blue eyes that beckoned so enticingly. Her lips were moist and rosy, still parted as if she would resume the kiss. He felt like he'd been kicked. Tenderly he cupped her face, rubbing gently over her lips, feeling the dampness on his thumb.

"This is not a good idea, Angel."

"It feels good to me," she said softly, her hand threaded in his thick hair. She could feel the pounding of his heart against her breast. It matched the tempo of her own.

"Your brother was right. I'm not the man for you."

"My brother?" The mood shattered. What was Jake talking about? "What brother? What did he say?" She pulled back and stared at him, puzzled and confused. When had either of her brothers even met Jake, much less spoken to him? What *was* he talking about?

"Never mind." He straightened, his expression instantly remote, forbidding. "If you can get yourself to bed all right, I'll leave. I'll be here tomorrow at three."

"Jake . . . ?"

"Good night." He closed the door behind him before she could ask another question. Damn, he'd blown that. He had never wanted her to know. Not that she still knew anything. He would not let his guard down in the future. Tomorrow he'd take her to the movie. Then Monday they'd review the grade sheets. If she could pick out a student whose grades were changed, they'd have a further lead. If not, he'd turn the entire investigation back to Pete Winston.

Pete was the officer of record. He should be doing the work.

Jake sat in the car until the lights went off in her house. Pulling away from the curb, he wondered why he didn't just turn the investigation back to Pete immediately. He could handle things. And Jake feared he might not be able to handle his own feelings much longer.

Angelica climbed into her bed, the past few minutes of the evening replaying in her mind. What had Jake meant about her brother? Which one? Rafe? Kyle? To her knowledge, neither knew Jake. Tomorrow she'd demand some answers. He couldn't casually slip something like that into a conversation and then ignore it.

Anger began to build. Which brother had told Jake he was not the man for her? And why? How could Jake have bought into the idea? It was obvious he agreed. He was not the only one looking for answers tomorrow. She'd find a few for herself!

One look at Jake's face the next afternoon, however, and Angelica knew she wasn't going to get a quick answer to her question. He looked angry and mean and loaded for bear. She had taken pains in dressing. She considered this a date even if he didn't. The dark wool slacks hugged her hips. The pink sweater was old, one she'd had for years, but he had said he liked it once. For that alone, she'd wear it till it hung in tatters.

"You always smell like honeysuckle," he said when he helped her on with her jacket, his knuckles brushing against her jaw.

"You make it sound like a crime." She reached up to flip out her hair, trying to match his casual tone.

Her skin tingled where he'd touched her. Her heart raced, and breathing became a chore.

His hand brushed over the shiny waves, lingering on the ends as he rubbed them gently between his fingers. "It's not a crime." His low voice washed through her like hot wine, smooth, soothing, delighting every nerve ending.

She didn't bring up the question in the car, though her curiosity almost raged out of control. Once they reached the theater, she wished she had. In the center of the lobby stood Jason Hunter and a young woman. Once they spotted Jake and Angelica, they hurried over.

"Greetings. Thought we'd see the movie with you. That way I can point out the social aspects I was discussing last night," Jason boomed heartily. He quickly introduced Liza Nesbet, his girlfriend, then turned with a friendly grin to Angelica. "You should injure yourself more often. Since I've known you, I've never seen you out and about as much since that happened."

She smiled politely, seething inside. She didn't want to share Jake with these two acquaintances. She had planned on the two of them spending the afternoon together. And maybe the evening. She wasn't going to let the day go by without finding out what he'd meant by that statement he'd let slip last night.

"Popcorn, no butter, and a cherry cola?" Jake asked Angelica as he ushered her across the lobby toward the concession stand. His hand was warm against the small of her back.

Giving into temptation, she slowed her pace to keep his hand firmly in place. As she turned slightly to smile up at him, it felt almost as if he were embracing her, his arm touching her shoulders, her back, his hand firmly guiding her.

She nodded. He remembered. After two years and who knew how many other women, he remembered what she liked at the movies. For a second, she remembered Diane, the woman he'd taken out at New Year's. He seemed to be neglecting her. He was spending too much time with Angelica to have any time to date Diane.

Feeling inexplicably better, Angelica resigned herself to a shared afternoon. But later, she'd get Jake alone and question him about that curious statement he'd made.

The movie was fun. Despite her earlier misgivings, Angelica enjoyed Jason's comments and the rude retorts his girlfriend made to put down his pretensions. They complemented each other, and at one point Angelica wondered what they thought of her and Jake. Did they complement one another?

He sat beside her, but made no move to hold her hand or put his arm around her shoulders. He held the popcorn in his lap, and she snuggled closer, ostensibly to better reach the snack.

Mingling with the aroma of the freshly popped corn was Jake's own scent, tangy and masculine, uniquely his. She longed to dash the bag from his hand, knock over the drinks and crawl into his lap. Did anyone ever do that in the movie theater? Would she be starting a trend? Or causing a scandal? She could see the headlines in the *Daily Bugle*. Math Professor Shocks Theatergoers With Wanton Behavior. She sighed and reached for some more popcorn. It would never happen, but she wished she dared.

Jason and Liza suggested dinner. Jake concurred with unflattering alacrity. While they discussed a place, he suggested a grill down on Third Street. "It's a cop hangout, but I think you'd like it," he explained, glancing down at Angelica.

Saying nothing, she nodded. Two years ago, he had not taken her to any cop hangouts. They had gone to dinner in Cheyenne, down in Fort Collins, even at that trendy place on First Street. But none of them had been a cop hangout. Why now?

Jake was well liked. That much was evident from the men and women who greeted him when he walked into the grill. Several came over to visit briefly when they were seated. Jason and Liza joined in the conversation as if they'd been longtime friends with everyone, and more and more chairs were dragged up, crowding their table. Angelica said very little, watching the activity. Jake deliberately put up barriers. Why?

When a pert and friendly red-haired woman joined them, Jake introduced her as Diane Waters. Angelica's attention immediately focused on the woman. This was Diane? She was adorable.

Gritting her teeth, she wanted to go home. She didn't need this. At the first break in the conversation, she glared at Jake. "I have a headache. Do you think you could take me home and then come back?"

"Have something to eat first. It'll make you feel better."

"The service here isn't the greatest, but the food is wonderful," Diane said genially. She leaned over Jake and hugged him. "I haven't seen you in a coon's age. Where have you been? Up at your cabin?"

He nodded. "Fixing it up some."

"When do I get to see it?" she asked, her bright, bubbly enthusiasm almost more than Angelica could bear. She stood up and walked out.

Once on the sidewalk, she looked down the street. It was too far to walk home, she knew, not with her ankle. Otherwise she might try it. The wind blew from the west, chilling her to the bone. She had to find a phone and—

"What the hell do you think you're doing?" Jake asked, pulling her around, clamping his hands on her shoulders in a hard grip. He was angry, his eyes blazing down on her.

"I'm going home. I told you I had a headache."

"If you would eat something besides popcorn, you'll feel better."

"When I need a mother, I'll let you know. I want to go home." She knew she sounded childish, but she couldn't help it. She just wanted to be away from this place, away from his friends, away from Diane.

"Too good for the grill? These people not intellectuals like you're used to at your fancy university? Too common?" he snarled.

She blinked at the attack, staring up at him. Was that really how he interpreted her actions?

"It's not that," she said, suddenly feeling guilty. She really hadn't given them a chance. But she didn't want to be around Diane. It was too painful.

"It sure looks like it. Where are your manners? Certainly you can bear up long enough to eat. After all, Jason and Liza are here. They're from your world. Talk to them if that makes you feel any better."

"It's not that," she mumbled. Her gaze dropped to his chin. She couldn't tell him. Yet she didn't want him to think she was such a snob that she didn't like his friends, his co-workers.

"What is it, then?" He leaned over until his nose almost touched hers, his hand beneath her chin, tilting her face to meet his. "If it isn't that, what is it?"

She didn't want to have to say it. It made her seem so petty. But it was true.

"I'm jealous," she whispered.

"What? Are you nuts?"

She shook her head, embarrassment flooding her.

He cupped her chin and his thumb caressed her jaw. She hated looking at him, afraid of the disgust she'd see, or the laughter.

But she saw only bafflement.

"Why are you jealous? Or is the question who are you jealous of?"

"Whom."

"Angel."

"Diane."

He stared down at her for long moments. The wind whipped around them, cold and harsh. Angelica didn't feel it. The heat of embarrassment threatened to consume her. She didn't want to feel this way. He'd made it clear there was no future in a relationship between them. And he was certainly free to see anyone he wanted. But she did feel jealous. She bitterly resented the fact he had invited Diane to spend New Year's Eve with him. Bitterly resented the fact he'd been dating while she had been so lonely since he'd gone. Bitterly resented the fact she loved a man who didn't love her in return.

"Angel, Diane is a friend. She works in dispatch and sometimes we go out. Just for fun. There's no need for you to be jealous of her or anyone else.'' His voice was soft and husky.

"Jake?'' Jason peered around the door. Laughter and light spilled from the opening. "Is everything okay?''

"Yes. The cold air cured her headache. We're coming back in now,'' Jake said, his eyes never leaving Angelica's.

"The waiter is finally ready to take the orders.''

"We'll be right there.''

The door closed and they were alone on the sidewalk again.

"Coming?'' he asked softly.

"What, refuse to return and make a cop out to be a liar?'' she asked. Her heart ached, but there appeared to be nothing to do but go on with the evening.

Angelica was relieved to find Diane had left the group by the time she and Jake returned. Once dinner arrived, the others drifted away until only the four of them remained at their table. Despite the rocky beginning, she relaxed and began to enjoy herself. Jason and Liza were a funny couple, had been together for several months and were discussing marriage. This was from Jason; Liza kept flirting with him, yet holding him off.

When she and Angelica went to the rest room at one point, Liza admitted she was crazy for the guy. "But I don't want him to become too complacent; even after we marry. How will he appreciate me if I fall too easily?''

Angelica nodded, but wondered if she could ever play games like that. She would want her husband as secure in her love as she would wish to be in his.

When they finished eating, Jake asked if she wanted to leave. She shook her head. She was having fun.

Again the numbers at the table swelled. Jason was in seventh heaven, arguing social problems with cynical policemen. Jake leaned back and watched Angelica discussing the current university art exhibit with Sergeant Leroy Burns. Leroy's hobby was oil painting and he and Angelica compared reactions to the exhibit.

It was late when they left.

"I liked your friends," she said with a yawn as he settled her in the car.

"Good."

She was pleasantly silent during the drive. The evening had turned out much better than she had thought at the beginning. Diane had not reappeared, and that helped.

When Jake stopped the car at her place, she turned her head against the back of the seat and looked at him. "Which brother did you talk to and what did you two discuss?" she asked. She couldn't let the evening end without knowing. She suspected it might be important.

"Drop it, Angel. It's old news and changes nothing. I'll pick you up at 7:30. Will that give you enough time to get to your early class?"

Just a week ago, they'd returned from the mountains for her early class. It seemed longer. That carefree weekend seemed a lifetime in the past. Tomorrow, it was back to school, and this time she would take the elevator. If Jake offered to escort her to her office and then her first class, she wouldn't refuse.

"Jake, I want to know," she insisted.

He opened his door and walked around to open hers. "Sometimes we don't always get what we want," he said as he helped her out onto the sidewalk. "Give me your keys and let's get inside. It's cold."

"Are you coming in?" she asked, shivering as she waited for him to unlock her door and turn on some lights.

"Not tonight. It's late and you have an early class. I'll see you in the morning." He brushed his fingertips down her cheek and turned toward his car.

Angelica watched until he drove away. Turning off the living room lights, she wandered into her bedroom, frustrated with Jake's refusal to answer her question. She knew she could question him from now until the cows came home, and if he chose not to respond, he wouldn't.

"There are always ways to find things out, Mr. Hotshot Detective. You are not the only one who can interrogate people. If you won't tell me, I'll find out from the source."

It was too late to call either of her brothers. But before the week was out, she vowed she would talk to both of them and find out which one had talked to Jake and what had been said.

Jake picked her up the next morning, placed a police emblem on his dash and parked in her slot at the university. He walked her to class, then headed for the administration building. By noon they were both in her office, reviewing the grades of her fall-semester classes.

"Honestly, I can't remember," Angelica said, studying the list. "Wait, this is odd. Jim Smithers should have had an A. I know that much. He received an almost-perfect score on the final. But it shows up as a C." She made a notation beside the grade.

"Which class?"

"Calculus, Tuesdays and Thursdays. Umm, I think Janey did better than a C, too. Wait a minute. This is wrong. Peggy Albert failed the course. Yet this printout shows a C. I know she failed because she's on a scholarship and I hated to have to give a failing grade, but she didn't do the work and failed all the tests. Her final exam score was higher than anything she'd done all year, but not enough to raise the grade."

"So three students that you can remember now have different grades. Two lower than you remember, one higher," Jake summarized.

She nodded, studying the lists. Frustrated not to have her grade book, she tried to recall what each student had earned. Shaking her head in defeat, she looked up. "That's the best I can do. Where are the lists I sent into administration?"

"Apparently they keep them for a week after they send the grades out for verification, then toss them."

"Well, the university would be swamped with paper if it kept every piece," she said reasonably.

He stood and took the list she'd marked. "I'll give these to Pete. He can start checking. We'll start with the students in this class. Two are girls. The one male you marked would be crazy to lower his grade."

"Plus Jimmy is not even as tall as I am. I can't see him as the man on the stairs."

"I'll let you know if we turn anything up." He sketched her a small salute and headed for the elevators.

Was that it? If he found who had committed the crimes, he'd just let her know? And how did he plan to do that? Drop her a note in the mail?

Slowly she drew her phone close. Time enough to worry about that later. Right now, she had some calls to make. She would start with Rafe. Before the day was over, she would have some answers.

The sun hovered just above the Snowy Range Mountains by the time Angelica turned onto the long road that led to the Rafter C. Rafe had been no help. That left Kyle. Suspecting her bossy brother had interfered where he had no business being, she decided to confront him face-to-face rather than talk to him over the phone.

It had been several months since she'd been home and she felt the same surge of satisfaction and delight she always felt when on the Rafter C. You could take the girl off the ranch, but you couldn't take the ranch out of the girl. No matter how much she enjoyed teaching, she always felt at home here. Suddenly she was anxious for summer to return. She usually spent a few weeks in July riding, helping with the chores, renewing herself.

Kyle was out when she arrived. It would be dark in another hour or so. He'd be back by then. She let herself into the house, shaking her head at the mess in the kitchen. Since their former housekeeper had left to take care of her invalid mother, Kyle had not been able to keep a replacement. And if anyone needed someone else to do housekeeping chores, it was her brother!

She wandered around the house, adrenaline pumping. She wanted to get some answers. Where was he? Time would pass faster if she were busy. So thinking, she rolled up her sleeves and headed for the kitchen.

"Angel! I didn't know you were coming."

Kyle entered the kitchen two hours later. Tall and lean, he looked tired and dusty. Shedding his shearling jacket and cowboy hat, he gave his sister a quick hug. When he glanced around the kitchen, his face lit up in a genuine smile.

"Thanks for cleaning up. And—" he drew in a deep breath "—from the tantalizing aroma coming from the oven, I'd say I'm more than glad you came by. What did you fix?"

"Meat loaf. You didn't have anything else. When are you going to replace Rachel and get another housekeeper?"

"I'm trying. Is it my fault none of the ones the agency sends out will stay? Who would want to come to work on a remote ranch in the dead of winter? The last one only left a couple of days ago. I'll get someone out soon. What's the occasion for the visit? What's happened? How did you get hurt?" he asked, spotting the support on her ankle.

"It's a long story. I'll tell you over dinner." And get a few answers in exchange!

CHAPTER TEN

THEY fell into a familiar routine. Angelica served up dinner; Kyle set the table. It reminded Angelica of evenings when she was growing up, after her parents had died. For so long it had just been Kyle, Rafe and her. Suddenly she was afraid. She didn't want her brother to have done anything that would alter their relationship. Glancing at Kyle, she hesitated, then decided to withhold her questions until after they ate. No sense in ruining the meal she'd prepared. Time enough for indigestion when they were finished.

As they began to eat, she explained how she had hurt her ankle.

"And the police haven't found out who did it yet?" he said, scowling.

She smiled at his expression, it was so similar to Jake's. While her brother had the same fair hair and light eyes that she had, his features were rugged and masculine. He was just as quick to jump to her defense as Jake.

"They're working on it. They think they'll find the man soon."

"You should move back home until they do," he said firmly.

"My home is in Laramie," she said easily, trying to keep the sudden flash of anger under control. She was not Kyle's baby sister anymore; she was all grown up.

"Here, I mean."

"I know, Kyle, but I'm a big girl now. I can take care of myself. And I live in Laramie. That's my home now."

"Someone should be watching out for you."

She smiled again, he sounded so much like Jake. Where had she gone wrong in her life that she gave these men the impression she could not take care of herself? Did all sisters go through this? she wondered.

"Someone is looking out for me," she replied.

"Seeing someone special?" he asked, putting down his fork to study her.

"No. No one special." She paused and took a deep breath. This was it. "Actually, no one at all."

"What do you mean?" He pushed away his empty plate and stared at her, puzzled.

"I mean, I haven't been seeing anyone at all in over two years."

He leaned back in his chair, his eyes never leaving hers. "Two years?"

"Uh-huh. Two years. Shall I tell you about it?" she said, her voice deceptively calm. She leaned forward, anger coloring her cheeks, her eyes flashing blue fire. "Two years, one month, and twenty-three days. But who's counting?"

"Angel—" He began frowning.

"Two years ago, I was dating a wonderful man. I was crazy about him. Absolutely top over tail in love. I've never been in love before, but I knew it was the real thing. I love him. Then I went to Rafe and Charity's that first Thanksgiving, right after they were married. When I returned to Laramie, this man I love never called again. I called him, but he brushed me off."

"Angel—"

Ruthlessly she continued, not giving Kyle a chance to say a word. "I never knew why. So we stopped seeing each other. I could have dated other men, but I knew that I didn't care to spend my time with anyone else. I didn't want to date. I didn't want to search for another man to fall in love with. It would never be the same. I love Jake Morgan. I loved him then, I love him now. I will love him until the day I die."

"Oh, God," Kyle said, rubbing his hand over his face, meeting his sister's eyes again, as if compelled to do so.

"Right. I've been desperately unhappy for a long time, Kyle. And you know what? I just found out something that leads me to suspect you had something to do with that unhappiness." She wanted to throw something to relieve the escalating tension. She stared at her brother, willing him to refute her charge. Willing him to say he hadn't a clue what she was talking about.

He stared at his sister for a long moment. "I meant it for the best," he said at last.

"Whose best? Yours? Certainly not mine." Tears shimmered in her eyes. She had so hoped she was wrong, that neither of her brothers had done anything so horrible. "Kyle, I have been desperately unhappy for over two years. I tried to hide it so you and Rafe wouldn't worry. I didn't want you to. There was nothing you could do, I thought. Now I want to know exactly what happened. What did you do? And why?" She took a deep breath, trying to calm the raging turmoil. *What had her brother done?*

"Angel, the man's a cop. You know how dangerous that kind of life is?"

"That's it? You don't like him because he's a cop?"

"It's a dangerous life. I want someone better for you. Someone who wouldn't cause you to worry about his safety your entire life."

"Is being a cop more dangerous than being a cowboy? More dangerous than a rodeo rider? Give me a break. It's not any more dangerous than a lot of professions. What am I supposed to do? Wait for a man who has a perfectly safe job, huh, Kyle? And then make sure he never leaves the house in case a car careers out of control and kills him?" she asked sarcastically. Their parents had been killed in just such a manner. "What did you do, Kyle? Besides ruin my chance for happiness. I want to know what you did."

He shoved back his chair and paced over to the counter, leaning on his hands and gazing out the window into the dark yard. "Not that much. If he had cared for you, he would have told me to go to hell and gone on seeing you. I called him, and he backed off."

"I want to know what you told him." She was feeling sick. Her brother had warned Jake off. She still couldn't believe it.

"I told him to stay away from my baby sister. That's what." Kyle slammed his hand down on the counter and turned. "Someone has to watch out for you, Angel. You are too easy to take advantage of. You have a lot of money behind you. This ranch does very well. I wanted to make sure he wasn't some fortune-hunting opportunist looking for a free ride. Cops don't make a lot of money."

"I don't believe it." She stood and limped over until she faced Kyle. Angrily she poked his chest with her index finger, rage threatening to make her lose all self-control. "Just because Jeannie tried to take you for all you had doesn't mean everyone else in the world is cut from the same cloth. Just because your fiancée was a fortune hunter doesn't mean any man who was interested in me would be. Damn you, how dare you interfere with my life?''

''I dared because I was worried about you.''

''I'm a grown woman, perfectly capable of choosing my own mate in life. I don't need or want any interference from my brother. Just because you were born a couple of years before me doesn't give you any rights over me, now or in the future. It's none of your business whom I see, whom I date or whom I marry. You got that clear, cowboy?''

''Angel, I did it for you, to protect you.''

''No! I don't know why you ever thought you had the right to interfere in my life, but you were not doing it for me. I don't need your protection! Was it a power trip, or just jealousy that your brother and sister had both found someone special and you were alone? Or were you just lashing out wherever you could because of Jeannie?''

He stared at her, grabbing her hand and holding it away from his chest. ''Leave Jeannie out of it. She had nothing to do with it. I thought you and Tom Bolton might make a go of it,'' he retorted. ''He's got his own spread now. You and he were always close. At least I know he's not some fortune hunter.''

''I could scream. Tom and I were friends when we were in *high school*. I haven't seen him in years. In case it escapes your attention, my life is now in Laramie, at the university. I would no more want to marry a rancher than I would want to be one.'' The enormity of what her brother had done was almost too much to grasp. "Did you tell Jake I was seeing someone else?"

"Damn it, Angel, I told the man you were practically engaged to a man you'd known all your life. I told him you might be having a fling with him, but when the time came to marry, he wasn't even in the running."

"I don't believe it. Kyle, you bastard!" She took a deep breath, the hurt almost too deep to bear. She had expected support from her brothers, not this. "You stay out of my life from now on, is that clear? I don't want to see you again. I don't want to talk to you ever again. *Stay out of my life*!"

She snatched her hand away and stomped over to the coatrack. Yanking her jacket down, she donned it and turned.

"Angel, I'm sorry. I didn't know your feelings went so deep," he said, leaning against the counter, his expression contrite and sincere.

"Sorry isn't good enough, Kyle. You never asked, did you? You just took charge and tried to run my life. I don't know if I'll ever forgive you for this. I have spent the past two years alone. Maybe I'll spend the rest of my life alone because of your blasted interference. Stay away from me from now on!"

She almost ran to her car, ignoring the twinges of pain each step shot through her ankle. Kyle appeared in the back door as she started her engine. She put her car in gear and gunned it, gravel spurting beneath her wheels. She was almost shaking with reaction. She felt sick. For a moment, she considered pulling off to the side of the road just in case. Swallowing hard, she pressed on.

She wasn't sure how she was going to handle matters with Jake, but she would set him straight on a few things the next time she saw him. She also knew it would be a long time before she got over her anger with Kyle. Or the sense of betrayal she felt. A very long time, if ever.

When she reached home, some of the tension had abated. There was a message on her answering machine from Jake asking her to call him. She tried immediately, but he was not at home. Slowly she replaced the receiver, relieved he hadn't answered. She didn't want to call him; she wanted to see him. Tomorrow. In the meantime, she had a lot to think about.

One thing Kyle had said echoed over and over. If Jake had really cared about her, he would have told her brother to go to hell and continued seeing her. But he had not. She didn't like the thought, but maybe Kyle was right. Maybe Jake really didn't care for her the way she wanted him to. Maybe he didn't love her the way she loved him.

Jake called just as she was dropping off to sleep.

"Where were you today?" he asked abruptly.

"I had errands to run," she replied vaguely. She was not going to tell him about Kyle over the phone. She wanted to talk to him face-to-face. Maybe then she'd find out how he really felt.

"Driving all right?"

"Yes. I didn't need my left foot, so I managed fine. I'm not using the cane anymore." She clutched the receiver tightly, wishing she knew what to do, what to say. Would Jake have stopped seeing her just on Kyle's say-so?

"So you don't need a ride in the morning?"

"No." She would like if he offered it anyway. Holding her breath, she waited apprehensively.

"What's your schedule tomorrow?"

"My first class isn't until ten, but I thought I'd go into the office around nine." She wanted to see him but was afraid. She would confront him with what Kyle had done, and then what? If her brother's comment was accurate, it would make no difference to Jake. Maybe he just didn't care enough for her.

"We think we have a lead. I'll speak to you tomorrow."

"Who?"

"Tomorrow." With that, he hung up.

Angelica glared at the phone as she slammed the receiver down. Blast the man, how did he expect her to sleep tonight worrying about whom they suspected? One of her students? Obviously, since it followed so soon after discovering the grades had been changed in her calculus class. But who?

Angelica dressed with care the next morning, trying to cover the dark circles beneath her eyes. She usually wore woolen slacks to work since it was so cold in winter. But today she chose a dusty pink woolen sweater paired with a dark brown skirt. She brushed her hair until it gleamed with highlights, applying enough makeup to hide the evidence of her sleeplessness. Dressing up had nothing to do with Jake's coming to see her today. She just wanted a change.

The morning dragged by. He did not come, or call, before her first class. She watched the back of the classroom during the hour, thinking he might drop in as he had before. He did not.

Working through lunch so she wouldn't miss him, she was beginning to worry when he finally showed up at her door.

"Hi." She looked up and smiled. Her heart raced and her hand grew damp. She had practiced what she would say when she saw him, but suddenly her mind went blank. All she could do was stare at him and feel the electricity sparking through her. Would she ever get tired of looking at him? Ever stop wanting him?

"Hi. Can I close the door?" he asked, cocking an eyebrow.

At her nod, he shut the door behind him and walked over to the chair across the desk from her.

"You found him," she said, noticing the seriousness of his expression.

"We found him. Alan Dalton. Know him?"

Slowly she shook her head. The name didn't ring a bell.

"Not surprising. He wasn't one of your students, though he does attend the university. He's Peggy Albert's boyfriend."

Instant understanding. "He changed her grade so she could keep her scholarship."

"Bingo. Apparently, without the scholarship she was out of school. Alan didn't want that for her, for himself."

Angelica frowned. "So he risked jail to keep her in school?"

Jake nodded. "That's it. We've got a complete confession—breaking and entering, vandalism, malicious mischief, assault and battery, tampering with the computer, theft." He shook his head. "He's twenty-one, studying computer science. That's how he knew how to break into the university computer and alter the grades. He switched more than one to confuse the issue if anyone suspected anything. Then he had to get your grade sheets to make verification that much more difficult.''

She sighed. ''All for his girlfriend.'' Idly she rubbed her sore wrist. What a sad ending for a young student with potential. ''And a girlfriend who wouldn't have been in that situation if she had just done the work. What a waste.''

''He said he was sorry for knocking you down. That was an accident. He only wanted to grab the briefcase and run.''

She nodded. If she hadn't lost her balance, she would not have fallen. It probably had been an accident. He hadn't deliberately pushed her.

''Now what?'' she asked.

''We're turning the case over to the D.A. His office will contact you. If there's a trial, it'll be in a couple of months. My guess is the kid will continue to admit he did it and there'll be a hearing and sentencing. But you don't have to worry anymore. The reasons for the break-ins are gone. He wanted your grade book, and when he couldn't find it in your house, he tried here, your car. Finally taking the briefcase where you kept it.''

She smiled shyly. ''Thank you for watching after me, Jake. You said you'd find the guy, and you did.''

He stood. ''Just part of the job.''

''Wait. I wanted to talk to you.'' Was he leaving? Just like that? The case was solved, so he was going?

Not if she had anything to say about it.

''About?'' He remained standing, looking as if he'd bolt at any moment.

"About my brother, Kyle. I went to see him yesterday."

Jake's expression didn't waver. He regarded her steadily as he stood before her desk. "And?"

"And he told me you two talked a couple of years ago." She pushed back her chair and stood. It helped shorten the distance she had to look up at him. If he wouldn't sit, she would stand.

Jake clenched his fists but remained silent. The betraying gesture touched Angelica. Taking heart, she walked around her desk, her ankle scarcely aching. She had expected a better reception than this. Rather, hoped for a better one. But she had always hoped around Jake. It didn't often do any good.

"Jake, I never knew why you stopped calling me. I thought we were having fun. I enjoyed spending time with you." She stopped close enough to him that she could feel his heat, breathe his after-shave.

"Your brother set me straight on a few things, that's all. He was right. You and I don't have much in common." His voice was carefully neutral.

"Are you nuts? We get along fine. More than fine most times." She reached out and touched his cheek lightly. His hand snapped up and grabbed her wrist, pulling her away from him, his fingers pressing into the soft skin like a band.

"What we had worked for a while. But Kyle was right. We are too different to make a go of it. I'm a cop, Angel. That's all I ever wanted to be. I make a good salary, but nothing to compare with the money you have from the Rafter C. And I'm old-fashioned enough to want to provide for my own family, not live off a rich wife. Besides, what happened to the man you were going to marry?"

The clenching of his teeth gave her a clue he was not as disinterested as his tone suggested. She took heart. "Jake, that's plain dumb. First of all, I'm not rich. Weren't you listening when I told you I finally could afford a town house because of my second job at the air force base? I don't have any money from the Rafter C. I'm part owner with Kyle and Rafe, but all the money is plowed back into the ranch. That's what keeps it going, keeps it up-to-date and modern. Secondly, there is no other man. There never was. Kyle made that up."

"My job's too dangerous," he continued as if she hadn't spoken. "I know from wives of other cops that they worry constantly about their husbands. Living with that kind of fear is draining."

She tugged at her hand, but he didn't release her, his grip tightening instead. "You're as bad as Kyle. No wonder you stayed away. You agree with him. Life is dangerous. No one gets out alive. I could have been killed if I had hit my head hard enough the other morning. But I wasn't. You could be killed in a car crash like my parents, or fall off a ladder like your uncle. Nowhere does it say that anything in life is guaranteed. Except I can guarantee you that I love you."

His lips moved in a semblance of a smile, but it didn't reach his eyes. "Hero syndrome. I saved you, so you're grateful."

"Grateful be damned! Let me tell you something, Jake Morgan." The index finger of her other hand poked his chest, just as she had done with her brother. These men made her so angry she could scream. "For the past two years, I have not had a single date. Do you want to know why?" Without waiting for him to reply, she continued, ''Because I didn't want to go out with anyone but you. I loved you then and I love you now. I've loved you all along. You may not love me, and if that's the way of things, I'll learn to cope. I had started to cope over the past few months, and I can do it again. But if you feel anything for me, tell me. Jake, I love you.''

He took her other hand and bent both behind her, pressing her body against his as he lowered his mouth to hers. His kiss was sweet. Gentle. Brief. Lifting up his head, he gazed down into her eyes for an endless moment as if imprinting her features in his mind for all time.

''You get on with your life, Angel. You've got a great future here at the university. You'll find a nice intellectual type to talk to and share your ideas with. I'm not for you, sweetheart, much as I wish I were. I don't know anything about family life. It was just my uncle and me for so long, then me alone. I'm a bad risk, any way you look at it. Listen to your brother, and me. Find someone else, Angel.''

He kissed her again, then released her and turned.

She stood stock-still, staring in disbelief as he opened the door and walked down the long hallway. She moved slowly to the doorway and watched as he pressed the button for the elevator, then was swallowed up inside as the doors closed behind him.

He'd gone. He had not said he loved her. He had not replied to her confession of love at all. Instead, he agreed with Kyle.

Her heart felt as if it were breaking. She raised her palm to her chest and pressed hard, trying to assuage the ache. She had counted on Jake loving her. She thought back over the past few weeks. He'd been so attentive. His kisses had melted all her resistance, and he had seemed to be struggling for control, as well. Had she totally misread the situation?

The elevator chimed. For one brief, heart-stopping moment, she thought he was coming back. Her heart soared. But two students stepped out and headed away from her. Sighing, she turned, closed the door behind her and let the tears fall.

Somehow, Angelica made it through the rest of the day. And for minutes at a time, she was able to forget Jake and the hopes she'd had of his admitting he loved her. Even walking to her car, she couldn't help glancing around, hoping to see him waiting for her. Looking over the area reminded her of how he always scanned the vicinity whenever they went anywhere. How long this time would it take to get her life under some sort of control? To regain the sense of contentment she'd begun to forge?

There were two messages from Kyle on her answering machine, both demanding that she call him as soon as she got home. The phone rang as Angelica was changing into jeans and she automatically reached for it. Would it be Jake? Hesitating, she didn't answer. Slowly she walked into her living room to listen to the message it recorded. Kyle again.

She turned the volume down and headed for the kitchen. Her head ached a bit. She'd fix a light dinner, then lie down. She sighed. She remembered last time she'd been so depressed that sleep had been her only panacea. Was she going to repeat that remedy?

Just after nine, her phone rang again. Angelica was lying on her bed, staring up at the ceiling. The hall light offered the only illumination. Slowly she reached out to answer the phone.

"Angel?"

"Hi, Rafe," she responded listlessly.

"What's up, baby sister?" he asked gently.

It was almost her undoing. Tears welled, but she fought to keep them from falling. Sitting up, she pushed her hand through her hair. "Life isn't much fun right now, big brother."

"So I hear from Kyle. You okay?"

"Do you mean physically or emotionally?"

"Both."

"My ankle still hurts a little. My wrist is almost well. My head aches tonight, but I'm not sure that's from the bump or the fact I told Jake I loved him today and he told me he wasn't right for me." She brushed the tears that spiked her lashes and took a deep, shaky breath.

"Is he right?" Rafe asked softly.

"No. But Kyle put the notion into his head and Jake's stubborn. I have to admit he can be as cantankerous as that old mule Daddy used to have. But I don't mind." She loved him happy, cranky, mad, stubborn. She wouldn't change anything except his answer that afternoon.

"And now you're mad at Kyle."

"You cannot even imagine how angry I am at him. He had no right to interfere with my life. I can manage things fine. If I mess up, I have only myself to blame. Except in this, I blame Kyle. I may never speak to him again. How could he do that to me?" Anger began to rise.

"He was just looking after his baby sister," Rafe explained.

"Ha. I'm only two years younger than he is. I don't need looking after. Rafe, I'm so lonely. I only want

to spend time with Jake. These past two years have
been hell. I keep as busy as I can with work and fixing
up this place, but it's not enough. Why can't he love
me back?''

"Maybe it's for the best— Wait a minute.''

"Angelica?'' Her sister-in-law's voice came across
the line.

"Hi, Charity.''

"Go away, Rafe. This is girl talk.'' There were
several seconds of silence, then Charity spoke again.
"Angelica, it seems to me these men have fouled
things up royally.''

Angelica smiled. Trust her petite sister-in-law to get
right to the heart of the matter. Her brother stood
well over six feet, yet his small, dark-haired wife had
him wrapped around her little finger.

"You could say that. I can't forgive Kyle for interfering. Nor Jake for agreeing with him.''

"You know your own mind, no matter what they
say. I think you'll forgive Kyle sooner or later. He is
your brother and his reason for interfering was sound,
even if misguided. The question I have for you is what
are you doing about the situation now?''

"What can I do? I told Jake I loved him, and he
walked away.''

"So you're just giving up?''

"I don't know,'' Angelica said.

"I'm going to tell you a secret that you are never,
never to let Rafe know you know.''

"Okay.''

"When we were first married, your stubborn
brother would not sleep with me. He was convinced
I went along with the marriage solely out of gratitude.
Stupid man, I was crazy about him from the first

moment I saw him, even if he was a rodeo cowboy. Anyway, that's why I was so delighted when you and Kyle came to spend that first Thanksgiving with us. With the two of you in the guest rooms, that left Rafe no place else to go but to my room!''

Angelica smiled. She could just picture Charity maneuvering her obstinate brother.

"So I get Jake over here somehow and force him into my bed?" she asked, trying to follow Charity's train of thought.

Charity giggled softly. "Maybe nothing that drastic. But you're a smart person. These men have no business making decisions for you. You make your own.''

"Charity, I owe you one. I've got an idea.''

"You owe me nothing. Just find your happiness like I found mine with your brother.''

Angelica hung up the phone a few minutes later, cheered beyond belief. Charity was right. There was no reason for her to let Kyle and Jake decide her fate. She was in charge of her life and she would live it as she wanted. And, if possible, with whom she wanted.

Returning to bed, she considered and discarded a dozen ideas. Finally, one came to mind that wouldn't be dislodged. She studied it from all angles. It would work. She would see that it worked. And if Jake didn't like it, well, too bad. Time he learned what it was like to have someone else make the decisions.

The next morning, Angelica called the police station and asked to speak to Pete Winston. After acknowledging she knew about the arrest and conferring about her testimony, she casually brought up Jake's name.

"He was such a help. Did he take the rest of his vacation time? I felt badly infringing on his free time," she said with false sincerity. She would infringe on his time from now on, whenever she had the chance.

"No. Came back to work yesterday. Should have taken the time off, though. He's as grouchy as a bear."

"The weekend's coming up. He'll get some rest then. He's not working an extra shift or anything, is he?" she probed.

"No, off from Friday night until Monday."

"I'm so pleased you found the man responsible," she concluded. She hoped Pete thought that was the only reason she called. She smiled when she hung up. Jake was in town and had the weekend free. Friday would be the day.

Angelica made her plans carefully. Thursday she drove by his apartment, studying the neighborhood. She stopped at four o'clock and parked in front of his building, watching the mothers walking their babies and the university students strolling home after classes. By four-twenty, the sidewalk was deserted.

Friday she shopped for groceries. Since Jake liked to eat and she liked to cook, she bought plenty of supplies. She wanted everything to be special. If they ran out, they could shop together.

She packed carefully, making sure she took the most obviously feminine apparel she owned. She added only a couple of jeans and T-shirts. She was out to make a statement, not blend in.

The hard part lay ahead. Actually, there were two critical times—the break-in and the confrontation. But she was determined to come out on top both times.

No more acquiescing to others. Charity was right. It was time she took charge of her own life.

She drove to Jake's apartment building and parked on a side street. Casually strolling along the sidewalk, she was relieved to notice how deserted the neighborhood was. It boded well for her plan.

Skirting the side of the building, she stopped beneath Jake's bathroom window, the one he always kept open. About four inches of clearance showed. She glanced around, her heart tripping in double time. Nervous in case of discovery, she was not truly afraid. If she was caught, she doubted he'd press charges. At least she hoped he wouldn't.

Dragging over a trash can, she carefully balanced on its top and stood, holding on to the side of the brick building. Reaching for the window, she pushed it all the way up. Taking a deep breath, she placed her hands on the sill and jumped. Her left wrist screamed in agony. Before she collapsed, she thrust herself through the window. Resting on her stomach, her legs dangling, she withdrew her hand and shook it to ease the pain. She had obviously overestimated the healing.

In only another minute, she stood in his tub. Peeking out the window, she verified the area was still deserted. She scanned the windows of the adjacent houses that overlooked this side of the apartment building. She saw no one. Lowering the window, she beamed with success. Stage one accomplished.

Within ten minutes, she had unloaded her car. Another half hour had her clothes distributed in his closet and dresser. She put away the groceries and started dinner.

When she heard the front door open, she held her breath. Slowly she turned from the stove and faced the living room. This was it. Jake walked in, paused, then looked at her, his dark eyes blazing, his body alert and poised as if for attack.

"What the hell are you doing here?" he demanded.

CHAPTER ELEVEN

"RIGHT here, right now?" she asked, stalling. "I'm cooking dinner." She took a deep breath and boldly walked over to him, holding eye contact the entire time. She could see the emotions dance across his face before he schooled his features. Daringly, she reached up and pulled his head down for a kiss.

His lips were cool, his cheeks cold. She opened her mouth and he responded instantly, his own moving possessively over hers as his arms drew her tightly against him.

Jake kissed her long and deep, breaking away only when breathing became difficult for both of them.

"What are you doing here?" He rested his forehead against hers, rubbing his nose against hers. His tone was soft, his eyes delving deep into hers.

"Cooking dinner?" she returned, hesitant to take the final step.

"And just how did you get in?"

She smiled saucily, her eyes dancing in delight. "There are always ways. Why doesn't the famous detective figure it out for himself?"

He thought a moment. "The bathroom window?"

She nodded. "For that you win the prize. Me." Reaching up, she brushed her lips across his again, then pulled back. "And dinner. I'm cooking beef Stroganoff. I made a deep-dish cherry pie for dessert." It was his favorite, that she remembered.

"Why are you here, Angel?" he asked as he shrugged off his jacket and tossed it across the sofa.

She turned back to the kitchen, keeping busy lest her courage fail. "For one thing, I wanted to see you again. For another, I thought a nice dinner would be a kind of thank-you for watching out for me while Alan was running amok."

"I don't need thanks."

"Right, you were only doing your job. I heard you say that the other morning. Maybe I want to cook dinner for you." Maybe do a lot of things for you.

"All right, then you go home."

"Actually, home is where your heart is. I have a house a few blocks over. But my home is here with you." She turned and faced him defiantly. "And here is where I'm staying."

He shook his head. "You can't stay here."

"Wanna bet? I've already moved in." She tilted her chin arrogantly. Curious to see what he would do next.

"What?" His voice was low, rough, angry.

"Check it out," she said flippantly, gesturing toward his bedroom.

In two seconds he was in the room; in ten he was back, anger radiating like an aura. "You can just pack up your things and get the hell out."

She smiled slowly, hoping she could camouflage the rapid beat of her heart. She dared not let him know how nervous she felt or she wouldn't stand a chance.

"Actually, I've decided I'm a bit tired of others running my life for me, so I thought I'd take over for a while. I'm twenty-six, you know, Jake. Don't you think it's time I was in charge of me?"

"I know how old you are. What does that have to do with anything?" He crossed the room until he crowded her into the kitchen.

She held her ground, refusing to back up or give way.

"It has to do with not needing anyone to tell me how to live or what's good for me. I don't need my brother choosing my boyfriends. I don't need the man I love acting like an altruistic damn fool and telling me what's good for me. I'm the only one who knows what's good for me. And I'm taking a stand tonight. Here I stay!"

He was silent, weighing her declaration, searching for something as he gazed deep into her eyes. He noted her determined stance, her stubborn chin and the fierce emotion reflected in her deep blue eyes. Slowly he nodded, reaching out to touch her skin, to feather his fingertips across her cheek, push her hair behind her ear, trace that strong jaw.

"Nothing's changed. I don't have a lot of money."

"Neither do I. I told you, the ranch takes back all the money it earns."

"I don't know much about family life. It was just my uncle and me, and he wasn't much on family stuff."

"I know lots, more than I want to sometimes, especially about nosy brothers who don't mind their own business. We can form our own family, make our own traditions and customs. You'll like Rafe and Charity. And right now, Kyle isn't a problem. I may never speak to him again."

"My job is still hazardous."

"So, apparently, is mine. When was the last time you were in the hospital? And didn't you tell me your uncle died off duty? I expect most cops retire and only a few die in the line of duty. We'll take our chances."

"Will we be able to blend our life-styles? I liked meeting your friends at the reception. Did you like my friends when we went out to dinner?"

Her gaze dropped to his chin. "Except for Diane," she mumbled.

He raised her head with his finger beneath her chin. "I told you there was nothing between us."

"I didn't come here to discuss your old girl-friends." She tossed her hair, waiting. *Waiting*.

"So you thought a fait accompli would accomplish what you wanted. Move in and leave me no choice?"

"You didn't give me any choice. You decided something was good for me and walked away. I think this is good for both of us and I'm not walking away." Could she pull it off?

"Your brother is right. You could do better than me."

"I don't think so."

Slowly he smiled, giving in. "All right. But on one condition."

She blinked, her heart threatening to burst. *All right*? He said it was *all right* that she move in with him? Happiness swept through her. She longed to throw herself into his arms, but caution held her back.

"What condition?" she asked warily.

"That we get married first," he said simply.

From walking away from her to marriage in one conversation was almost too much to take in! She stared, unable to breathe, unable to think.

Jake's smile broadened. His thumb brushed her lower lip, tugging gently. "Say yes," he urged, a moment of uncertainty setting in. Surely this was what she wanted. He knew beyond all doubt it was what he wanted.

"Yes," she repeated. "Are you sure?"

"Of what? That I want you to marry me? Yes, I'm sure. I was going to ask you two years ago, at Christmas. I thought that would be romantic. And I wanted to give you some romance. Then your brother stopped by on his way to Rafe's at Thanksgiving, and told me you were practically engaged to another man. The man was a rancher and you would be happier with someone you'd known all your life. Kyle let it slip that he suspected my motives were mercenary, that my job was too uncertain to offer stability to a woman like you. He said your family would not stand by if I continued seeing you. I guess I let pride and anger stand in the way of common sense. But you're right, Angel. You are grown. If you know what you want, who am I to say otherwise?"

"I sure hope there's something more," she murmured, stepping into his embrace, reveling in the feel of his strong body, the sensation of homecoming that was so strong.

"Like I love you, Angel? Like I've loved you for years, missed you so much I couldn't sleep nights."

"Something like that is nice," she nodded, resting her cheek against his. "Don't stop."

He chuckled as his hands traced the firm muscles of her back, rubbing up and down, pressing her breasts against his chest, her abdomen to his, her hips into his.

"How about I used to cruise down Sheridan Avenue when you lived in the apartment over there, just to see you start for school? How about I haven't been to Fort Collins since the day we wandered around there shopping, then had dinner at Antonio's? How about I'm only human and can stand only so much? There comes a time when a man knows when it's best to grab the future with both hands and hold on, whatever the risk."

"Umm, better and better." Happiness flooded her. Tears pricked. She burrowed closer, clinging. *Love you, love you, love you* her heart pumped rhythmically.

"How about I love you more than I thought it possible to love anyone? I want you more than anything." His low, sexy voice was intoxicating.

"I love you, too, Jake. I always have."

The time for talking was over. He kissed her.

The timer sounded for endless minutes before either recognized the sound.

"Dinner," she said, pulling away and turning to the stove.

"After dinner, we'll move your things back to your house."

She turned, stricken. "No, we won't. I told you I was staying, and I meant it."

"I said we'd marry first, and I meant it. Besides, I don't want your two brothers showing up and finding all your things at my place."

"Scared?"

"Yep."

She laughed at his teasing, wondering if Jake was ever afraid of anything. Except maybe committing his heart.

"I love you," she said clearly. She wanted to make sure he knew that for all time.

"I know you do. I love you. After dinner, I'll show you how much."

In the end, Jake had his way. They moved her things back to the town house later that evening.

"How attached are you to your apartment?" Angelica asked as they hung the last of her dresses.

"I've lived there for ten years, but it's only an apartment. Why?"

"Want to move in here?" she asked.

He looked around, then at her. "I could."

"Well, you're bringing the cabin to the marriage. I thought I could offer this."

"Are we bargaining?"

"Not really. I just don't want to live in an apartment again. I like my house. But if your pride demands that we live in your poky old apartment—"

He laughed, snatched her up and spun her around and around until she was dizzy. "I like this place, too. And no, my pride doesn't demand that we stay in my poky old apartment. It doesn't matter where we live at first, because before too long we are going to want a bigger place."

"We are?"

"For the kids."

Her heart melted. "Kids?"

"At least a half dozen," he said firmly.

"Wow, we'd better get started." Laughing happily, she tightened her arms around his neck and kissed him.

Charity Carstairs readjusted the skirt, settling the folds to her satisfaction. Standing back, she smiled at Angelica. "You look beautiful. Of course, I've never seen you when you didn't, but today especially so."

"Just as long as Jake thinks so," Angelica said, staring at herself in the full-length mirror. The long white dress was a dream. The lacy sleeves covered her arms to her wrists; the fitted bodice enhanced her slender figure. She could hear the organ playing softly, the murmur of the guests. In less than ten minutes she would walk down the aisle and marry Jake. She could hardly believe this was happening. It had been endless weeks since January. While she agreed six weeks wasn't too long to plan a wedding—scarcely long enough as it proved—she would have been satisfied with a quick marriage the week after he proposed. But Jake had insisted on a big wedding. They had invited almost the entire university staff and every law enforcement officer in the county. There were longtime family friends to be included, and the church was threatened with a standing-room-only crowd.

"Rafe's right outside. You ready?" Charity asked. She smoothed her own deep rose gown over her hips. She was Angelica's sole attendant.

"As I'll ever be." Angelica took a deep breath and reached for her bouquet. There was no reason to be nervous. She loved Jake, he loved her, and today they would join their lives together.

Charity opened the door and slipped out. Before it could close, Rafe and Kyle walked in together.

Angelica looked at her brothers, her expression wary when her gaze rested on Kyle.

"What are you doing here?" she asked.

"I've come to walk up the aisle with my brother to give my sister to the man she loves," Kyle said. "We're her only family right now, and we want to give her away together." Tension shimmered in the air as he waited for Angelica's response. The tightening of his jaw gave away the uncertainty he felt.

Angelica blinked back tears, pressing her lips together tightly so she wouldn't cry.

"I love you, Sis. I'm glad things worked out for you," Kyle added softly. "Despite the mess I made of things."

She reached out to hug him. Then turned to Rafe and hugged him, tears sparkling on her lashes.

"None of that." Rafe brushed the tears away. "We don't want everyone to think we're forcing you to marry the man."

"Or that you're having regrets," Kyle said, smiling warmly at his younger sister.

"I'm so happy today. Be happy with me," she whispered, love for both her brothers almost matching the love she had for Jake.

"We are," Kyle answered. "We are. Now the question is, can Jake ride?"

"Who cares? We're not living on a ranch. We're living right her in Laramie."

"Weekends?" Rafe asked.

"At our cabin in the mountains."

"Summers?" Kyle asked.

''Well, we'll visit once in a while, but our future is here. And mine is with him.'' Of that there was no doubt. She loved Jake, always had, always would.

The organ music changed.

''Time to go, Angel.''

Linking her arms with those of her two tall brothers, she smiled radiantly and started down the aisle to meet Jake. As he waited, his dark eyes caught hers and held as she walked steadily toward him and their future.

* * * * *

Look out for Barbara McMahon's next
WESTERN WEDDINGS book,
Kyle Carstairs' story in *Bride on the Ranch*,
a Mills & Boon romance,
available in paperback in April 1997.

As Seen on TV!

Free Gift Offer

With a Free Gift proof-of-purchase
from any Harlequin® book, you can receive
a beautiful cubic zirconia pendant.

This stunning marquise-shaped stone is a genuine cubic
zirconia—accented by an 18" gold tone necklace.
(Approximate retail value $19.95)

Send for yours today...
compliments of ◈ HARLEQUIN®

To receive your free gift, a cubic zirconia pendant, send us one original proof-of-
purchase, photocopies not accepted, from the back of any Harlequin Romance®,
Harlequin Presents®, Harlequin Temptation®, Harlequin Superromance®, Harlequin
Intrigue®, Harlequin American Romance®, or Harlequin Historicals® title available in
February, March or April at your favorite retail outlet, together with the Free Gift
Certificate, plus a check or money order for $1.65 u.s./$2.15 can. (do not send cash) to
cover postage and handling, payable to Harlequin Free Gift Offer. We will send you the
specified gift. Allow 6 to 8 weeks for delivery. Offer good until April 30, 1997, or while
quantities last. Offer valid in the U.S. and Canada only.

Free Gift Certificate

Name: _____

Address: _____

City: _____ State/Province: _____ Zip/Postal Code: _____

Mail this certificate, one proof-of-purchase and a check or money order for postage
and handling to: HARLEQUIN FREE GIFT OFFER 1997. In the U.S.: 3010 Walden
Avenue, P.O. Box 9071, Buffalo NY 14269-9057. In Canada: P.O. Box 604, Fort Erie,
Ontario L2Z 5X3.

FREE GIFT OFFER   084-KEZ
ONE PROOF-OF-PURCHASE
To collect your fabulous FREE GIFT, a cubic zirconia pendant, you must include this
original proof-of-purchase for each gift with the properly completed Free Gift Certificate.

084-KEZ

HARLEQUIN ROMANCE'S 40TH ANNIVERSARY SWEEPSTAKES
OFFICIAL RULES—NO PURCHASE NECESSARY

To enter, complete an Official Entry Form or 3" x 5" card by hand printing the words "Harlequin Romance's 40th Anniversary Sweepstakes," your name and address thereon and mailing it to: In the U.S., Harlequin Romance's 40th Anniversary Sweepstakes, P.O. Box 9076, Buffalo, NY 14269-9076, or in Canada to Harlequin Romance's 40th Anniversary Sweepstakes, P.O. Box 637, Fort Erie, Ontario L2A 5X3. Limit: one entry per envelope, one prize to an individual, family or organization. Entries must be sent via first-class mail and be received no later than 7/31/97. No liability is assumed for lost, late or misdirected mail.

Prizes: 150 autographed hardbound books (value $9.95 each U.S./$11.98 each CAN.). Winners will be selected in a random drawing (to be conducted no later than 8/29/97) from among all eligible entries received by D. L. Blair, Inc., an independent judging organization whose decisions are final.

IF YOU HAVE INCLUDED THREE HARLEQUIN PROOFS OF PURCHASE PLUS APPROPRIATE SHIPPING AND HANDLING ($1.99 U.S. OR $2.99 CAN.) WITH YOUR ENTRY, YOU WILL RECEIVE A NONAUTOGRAPHED 40TH ANNIVERSARY COLLECTOR'S EDITION BOOK.

Sweepstakes offer is open only to residents of the U.S. (except Puerto Rico) and Canada who are 18 years of age or older, except employees and immediate family members of Harlequin Enterprises, Ltd., their affiliates, subsidiaries, and all other agencies, entities and persons connected with the use, marketing or conduct of this sweepstakes. All federal, state, provincial, municipal and local laws apply. Offer void wherever prohibited by law. Taxes and/or duties on prizes are the sole responsibility of the winners. Any litigation within the province of Quebec respecting the conduct and awarding of a prize in this sweepstakes may be submitted to the Régie des alcools, des courses et des jeux. All prizes will be awarded; winners will be notified by mail. No substitution for prizes is permitted. Odds of winning are dependent upon the number of eligible entries received.

Any prize or prize notification returned as undeliverable may result in the awarding of that prize to an alternative winner. By acceptance of their prize, winners consent to use of their names, photographs or likenesses for purposes of advertising, trade and promotion on behalf of Harlequin Enterprises, Ltd., without further compensation unless prohibited by law. In order to win a prize, residents of Canada will be required to correctly answer a time-limited, arithmetical skill-testing question administered by mail.

For a list of winners (available after September 30, 1997) send a separate stamped, self-addressed envelope to: Harlequin Romance's 40th Anniversary Sweepstakes Winners, P.O. Box 4200, Blair, NE 68009-4200, U.S.A.

HR4ORULES

Happy Birthday to

Harlequin Romance®

With the purchase of three Harlequin Romance books, you can send in for a **FREE** hardbound collector's edition and automatically enter Harlequin Romance's 40th Anniversary Sweepstakes.

FREE COLLECTOR'S EDITION BOOK

On the official entry form/proof-of-purchase coupon below, fill in your name, address and zip or postal code, and send it, plus $1.99 U.S./$2.99 CAN. for postage and handling (check or money order—please do not send cash), payable to Harlequin Books, to: In the U.S.: 3010 Walden Avenue, P.O. Box 9071, Buffalo, N.Y. 14269-9071; In Canada: P.O. Box 622, Fort Erie, Ontario L2A 5X3. Please allow 4-6 weeks for delivery. Order your **FREE** Collector's Edition now; quantities are limited. Offer for the free hardbound book expires December 31,1997. Entries for the Specially Autographed 40th Anniversary Collector's Edition draw will be accepted only until July 31, 1997.

WIN A SPECIALLY AUTOGRAPHED COLLECTOR'S EDITION BOOK

To enter Harlequin Romance's 40th Anniversary Sweepstakes only, hand print on a 3" x 5" card the words "Harlequin Romance's 40th Anniversary Sweepstakes," your name and address and mail to: "40th Anniversary Harlequin Romance Sweepstakes"—in the U.S., 3010 Walden Avenue, P.O. Box 9076, Buffalo, N.Y. 14269-9076; In Canada, P.O. Box 637, Fort Erie, Ontario L2A 5X3. No purchase or obligation necessary to enter. Limit: one entry per envelope. Entries must be sent via first-class mail and be received no later than July 31, 1997. See back-page ad for complete sweepstakes rules.

Happy Birthday, Harlequin Romance!

Official Entry Form/Proof of Purchase

"Please send me my **FREE**
40th Anniversary Collector's Edition book and enter me in
Harlequin Romance's 40th Anniversary Sweepstakes."

Name: _____

Address: _____

City: _____

State/Prov.: _____ Zip/Postal Code: _____

089-KEP

089-KEP